THE DIARY OF AN ORGANIST'S APPRENTICE

Dr T H Collinson

THE DIARY OF AN ORGANIST'S APPRENTICE
at Durham Cathedral
1871–1875

---

by Thomas Henry Collinson
the first organist
St Mary's Cathedral, Edinburgh 1878–1928

---

edited with notes by
Francis Collinson

with a Foreword by
The Duke of Buccleuch and Queensberry, KT

ABERDEEN UNIVERSITY PRESS

First published 1982
Aberdeen University Press
A member of the Pergamon Group

All net profits from this book are donated
to The Choral Scholarship Fund,
St Mary's Cathedral, Edinburgh

British Library Cataloguing in Publication Data
Collinson, Thomas Henry
The diary of an organist's apprentice at Durham Cathedral 1871–1875
1. Durham Cathedral 2. Organ
I. Title II. Collinson, Francis
786.5'092'4 ML628
ISBN 0 08 028461 2

PRINTED IN GREAT BRITAIN
THE UNIVERSITY PRESS
ABERDEEN

FOREWORD

In 1979 the great triple-spired Cathedral Church of St. Mary in Edinburgh celebrated its centenary.

In recognition of the important part music has always played in the life of the Church and the choir for which it has been justly renowned, the occasion was marked by the launching of an Appeal to build up a Scholarship Fund for young entrants to St. Mary's Music School, formerly the Choir School.

Now, a most happy sequel to that event is the publication of the diary of the Cathedral's first organist, Dr. T. H. Collinson. His son, Mr. Francis Collinson has, with great generosity, made the diary available, so that sales of this volume may augment the Scholarship Fund.

All lovers of ecclesiastical music will applaud this fine contribution, by a father and son, spanning the Cathedral's first century, to the encouragement of musical perfection throughout its second century.

Buccleuch and Queensberry.

The Duke of Buccleuch and Queensberry, KT

DRUMLANRIG CASTLE
THORNHILL
DUMFRIES-SHIRE

19 May 1982

CONTENTS

ILLUSTRATIONS

PLATES

PREFACE

I have long desired to see in print the boyhood diary of my father, Dr Thomas Henry Collinson, which he kept as a music apprentice at an early age at Durham Cathedral. This was some seven years prior to his appointment as the first organist and choirmaster of St Mary's Cathedral, Edinburgh in 1878 at the age of twenty.

The opportunity presented itself with the St Mary's Cathedral Edinburgh Centenary Appeal, issued in 1978 under the patronage of the Duke of Buccleuch. The object of the Appeal, connected as it is with the well-being of the choristers, and therefore of the music, of the Cathedral, could not have been dearer to my father's heart, for he was to become totally absorbed in and devoted to the work and interests of the Cathedral for the rest of his life, which coincided with the first fifty years of the Cathedral's existence. I am pleased therefore to be able to offer *The Diary of an Organist's Apprentice at Durham Cathedral,* with such royalties and profits as may accrue therefrom, as a contribution to the St Mary's Cathedral Edinburgh Centenary Appeal for the establishment of a Scholarship Fund for Choristers.

I have to thank His Grace, The Duke of Buccleuch and Queensberry, KT for his kind Foreword to the book.

Publication has not been achieved without the help and encouragement of many good friends, helpers and well-wishers, among whom I would particularly wish to acknowledge and thank the following:

My wife Elizabeth, for her unfailing encouragement and support.

The Very Revd Philip Crosfield, Provost of St Mary's Cathedral Edinburgh, whose immediate enthusiasm and whose remark that he found the Diary 'quite fascinating' provided the initial impetus to go ahead and seek a publisher; also for his bringing the project to the notice of the Cathedral Old Choristers Association, whose members have been so generous as to contribute a sum of money towards the cost of publication; Mr Dennis Townhill, MusB, FRCO, organist and choirmaster of St Mary's Cathedral Edinburgh for undertaking correspondence concerning the Diary with the Dean and Chapter Library, Durham, and with the editorial staff of the periodical *The Chorister*.

Margaret Grieve, Innerleithen, for typing out the manuscript of the Diary in its entirety, for the sheer pleasure of the task.

Janet Joy Foster, Bristol, for carrying out a great deal of personal research at Durham; for establishing good relations with the Cathedral authorities and civic archival authorities there on my behalf, for gaining their interest in the Diary, and for correcting the proofs.

The Dean of Durham, The Very Revd Dr Peter Baelz and Chapter, for permission to use photographs belonging to Durham Cathedral, and for their interest and general help; Mr Roger C. Norris, MA, Dean and Chapter Library Durham, for information about the personalities concerned with the Cathedral and Diocese of the period, and for the provision of photographs; Mr W. R. Wright, Parties Clerk, Visitors Office, Durham Cathedral, for sending informative publications regarding the Cathedral, its organ and peals of bells, for making and sending photocopies of excerpts from out-of-print guide books and histories of Durham, and for other help and information; Mr Richard Lloyd, MusB, FRCO, organist of Durham Cathedral, for information concerning the musical apprenticeship system at Durham, now done away with, and the present system of appointment of sub-organists at the Cathedral, and for other help.

Mr D. Butler, BA, County Archivist of Durham, and Mrs Ann Mitchell, First Assistant Archivist, for much information from the County Record Office Archives, including photocopies of excerpts from the files of the *Durham County Advertiser*; and the proprietors of that newspaper for permission to quote from these; Mr S. C. Dean, County Librarian, for information and for permission to reproduce photographs and pictures from the Library's collections; Mr Ian Nelson, Reference Librarian, Durham City Library, and Ms Mary Hodgson, Assistant Reference Librarian, for much help, and for providing photographs and engravings of Durham.

Mr Cuthbert Harrison, MBE, TD, FIMIT, FISOB, Chairman of Directors, Messrs Harrison & Harrison, Organ Builders, Durham, for information regarding the history of the Harrison family and Firm, and for permission to reproduce the nineteenth century engraving of the organ factory at Durham; Mr Laurence Elvin, FSA, FRHist.S, FRSA, author of *The Harrison Story*, for permission to quote from his book, and for his interest in the Diary and the Diarist; Lady Longland, member of the Harrison Family, for bringing Mr Elvin's book to my notice.

The National Library of Scotland for furnishing a copy of the Ordnance Survey map of Durham and its environs of the approximate period, with permission to reproduce this.

Mr G. F. Collie, CBE, Aberdeen, for his interest in the Diary and for his recommendation of it to the Aberdeen University Press; Mr Colin

MacLean, Publishing Director, the Aberdeen University Press, for personal searches in the George Washington Wilson Collection of Photographs for suitable pictures of the Cathedral and City of Durham, and for much technical help and advice; The University of Aberdeen for the provision of photographs from the above Collection, with permission to reproduce these.

All other kind friends who have helped and encouraged in various ways the project of publication of *The Diary of an Organist's Apprentice at Durham Cathedral*.

Finally I wish to express my most grateful thanks to Messrs William Grant & Sons Ltd, Distillers, for a most generous subvention towards the cost of publication.

Francis Collinson
Innerleithen
1982

INTRODUCTION

This is the personal account of how a musically gifted youth living over a hundred years ago set about to qualify himself in music, and to attain professional standards in his art when music-teaching institutions were not so numerous as they are now. The title of the book is mine; in actual fact the account bears as its heading the single word 'Diary'. It has been a precious possession of mine all my life. Now I venture to hope that as a step by step account of the long and arduous road to mastery of the art of music; of a clear vision throughout the diary of the goal ahead; of cheerful but modest confidence of the diarist's own progress in his task; and of final and satisfying achievement, the account may be of interest to a wider public, particularly to those who may be travelling the same road themselves, and to those also to whom music and all pertaining to it is of interest.

The writer of the diary was my father, Thomas Henry Collinson, later to hold the degree of MusBac Oxon, Fellow of the Royal College of Organists (*honoris causa*) and after his life had ended, the degree of DMus Edinburgh, also *honoris causa*, conferred, as only very rarely, posthumously.

In the year when the diary commences, 1871, now a hundred and eleven years ago, the only public music-schools in existence in the British Isles were the Royal Academy of Music in London[1] and the Royal Irish Academy of Music in Dublin.[2] There was also the Royal Military School of Music at Kneller Hall, Twickenham, Middlesex[3]; but this was solely concerned with the training of army bandsmen and bandmasters. In addition to these, there were of course the Faculties of Music at the ancient universities; but these were concerned with theory and musical composition rather than with the training of the executive musician; and the music degrees which they conferred were the accolade of the fully accomplished musician. Residence at a university was not in fact required in every case at this period because of the lack of adequate facilities for the actual teaching and study of music at many of our universities.[4]

One way to the study of music at the practical level was to serve an

1 Founded 1822.

2 Founded 1848.

3 Founded 1857.

4 Scholes, 'Degrees in Music' in *The Oxford Companion to Music.*

apprenticeship to the organist and choirmaster of one of the great cathedrals. This led naturally of course to a life of music in the service of the Church; and in those days there were few branches of the art of music in which a career of substance was more readily to be found in this country, provided that the musician could find himself in accord with this way of life. This was the way followed by my father; and the following pages contain the day-to-day diary which he kept meticulously, with but a few short lapses, throughout the four years of his apprenticeship. The place where he served his time was the ancient Cathedral of Durham; his master was the Organist and Master of the Choristers, Philip Armes, MusD *Oxon et Dunelm,* FRCO.[1]

The diary is, in practical terms, a day-to-day account; but I have reserved the editorial right to omit occasional entries which would seem to be of lesser interest. What gives the diary more than usual interest is the fact that the writer was only thirteen years of age when he commenced it. This was quite a usual age at which to be apprenticed to a trade or profession in one's own home town, but young perhaps to leave home and go to live in a strange city. As might be expected from the youthfulness of the writer, one finds the language refreshingly unsophisticated, particularly in the earlier pages;[2] and the impact of the great masterpieces of music, of Bach and Handel, Haydn and Mozart, Beethoven and Schubert (as well as the works of a number of lesser composers) is recorded, as these are unfolded in the diary's pages, through the eyes, or rather the ears, of keen and interested youth.

Thomas Henry Collinson, my father, was born at Alnwick, Northumberland, on 24 April 1858. His father, my grandfather, Thomas Collinson, was headmaster of the Duke's School, Alnwick[3]; a man much respected in that town, of whom the memory is still green, as I pleasurably found on a visit there only a year or two ago. The Diarist's mother, my grandmother, Hannah Sophia Gore, was before her marriage, schoolmistress of St Mary's School, Hastings, Sussex. On the fly-leaf of her beautifully printed and bound Book of Common Prayer, which I now possess and use, it is recorded that the book was presented to her at Hastings in July 1857, 'in grateful

[1] Philip Armes, born Norwich 1836; chorister at Norwich Cathedral and afterwards at Rochester Cathedral. Assistant organist of Rochester Cathedral. Organist of Holy Trinity Church, Gravesend, 1854; organist St Andrew's Church, Wells Street, London, 1857; Chichester Cathedral, 1861; Durham Cathedral, 1862–1907. Composer of oratorios, cantatas, church music, organ pieces, madrigals, etc. Cf. *Cathedral Organists*, John E. West (London 1899). A plaque in the cloister of Durham Cathedral says that Dr Armes was First Professor of Music at Durham.

[2] Wherever practicable I have retained in the text the grammar, spelling, punctuation and use of capitals as in the manuscript. F. C.

[3] The Duke's School, Alnwick was founded by the Duke of Northumberland in 1811 and maintained under the patronage of the successive Dukes.

acknowledgement of her valuable services and of her Christian character and conduct'. Hannah Sophia was my grandfather's second wife. His first wife, Mary Anne Rushforth died after only a few years of marriage, having borne him two sons, Frederick William (named after the German Kaiser) and Samuel. They were of course half-brothers to my father. They both appear frequently in the diary's pages.

A son, our Thomas Henry, my father, was born to Hannah Sophia and her husband; but alas, Hannah was to die after little more than two years of marriage. Thomas, my grandfather, was left with three young sons to look after, the youngest, Hannah's, being an infant of little more than one year old.

In due course my grandfather took the sensible step in the circumstances and married again. His third wife, Katherine Ann Sharpe, remained childless; but she was to prove a good and kind mother to the three boys. When my father refers to his mother in the pages of the diary, it is therefore his stepmother that is meant.

Thomas Henry Collinson, my father, became imbued from an early age with a love of music, a love which was coupled with an eager and somewhat unusual interest in the technique of its performance. He used to recount to us as children a memory of his own childhood at five years. It happened that the schoolhouse was being painted. My father, quick to seize an opportunity of receiving constructive criticism, sang a song to the painters, and then asked them for their opinion of his singing. One of the painters, of a jocular disposition, after a conventional word of praise, proceeded to inform him solemnly that a sure way of improving the voice was the swallowing of blackbirds' eggs! Thomas straightway went out into the schoolhouse garden, searched for and found a blackbird's nest, abstracted an egg and swallowed it. He then went back to the painter and sang the song again. The painter assured him that the quality of his singing voice had improved already!

Thomas's step-mother was his first music teacher, the musical instrument being the pianoforte. Her teaching abilities bore good fruit, and he made rapid progress in his playing. Discipline in his studies, probably initiated by his schoolmaster father, was strict but wholesome. Practice started before breakfast, at half past six in the morning, with scales and exercises.

At the age of nine, he commenced organ lessons under the local church organist, Charles Moore, organist at St Paul's Church, Alnwick, situated a few hundred yards from the schoolhouse. One year later, at the age of ten, he was proficient enough to play at the church service. His teacher, who was also the editor of the local newspaper, the *Alnwick Gazette*, has recorded that very soon he was able to deputise for him on the organ, and to take full charge of the music of the church service when required. More advanced organ lessons followed a little later from an organist of one of the churches in Newcastle-upon-Tyne, William Alphonse Leggat. These were supplemented with lessons in musical theory under a teacher resident in Alnwick, Mr I. M. Cramont.

Soon he was ripe for further advancement. His father arranged for him to be apprenticed to Dr Armes. At the age of thirteen he set off for Durham. A cutting from the *Alnwick Gazette* tells us that on his departure 'Master Thomas Collinson was presented by his fellow pupils at the Duke's School with an elegant Photographic Album'; and the report goes on to say that 'Master Collinson, as is well known, has already shown himself to be possessed of such singular musical talent as justifies us in auguring for him a successful and brilliant career'.

Arrived at Durham he found himself caught up at once and without preliminaries, in a microcosm of music-making and study that was to be his daily life for the next few years. This consisted firstly of his master and the two fellow apprentices who were to be his constant companions. Closely surrounding the little group was the circle with which the daily routine of the music of the Cathedral brought him in contact—the choristers, the clergy, in particular the Precentor, whose duties included the overall supervision of the music of the Cathedral services.

At a further remove from this circle were the organists and choirmasters of the other churches in Durham with whom the apprentices found themselves in frequent association, often assisting them or deputising for them when they had reached the required proficiency. It seems from the diary account that the Cathedral apprentices enjoyed more or less the freedom of the church organs in the city, to play on them and familiarise themselves with the different organ stops and their technical and tonal idiosyncracies, against the occasion when they might be called upon to play them at church service.

The most notable of these church organists of Durham was Dr J. B. Dykes of St Oswald's Church, a celebrated composer of hymn tunes. John Bacchus Dykes was in fact the vicar of St Oswald's and a minor canon of Durham Cathedral, and being both clergyman and musician, acted as his own organist as far as was practical. He was the composer of many well-known hymn tunes, some of them since become greatly loved, such as 'Nearer my God to Thee', 'The King of Love my Shepherd is', 'Through the night of doubt and sorrow' and 'For those in Peril on the seas'. My father came to be closely associated with him, and became his assistant organist before he had been in Durham many months. Towards the end of his apprenticeship, during the years of the last illness of Dr Dykes, he was appointed as official organist of St Oswald's. Within this same period he became also assistant organist of Durham Cathedral.[1]

[1] The exact date of his appointment as assistant organist at Durham Cathedral is not known to me. It receives confirmation in a letter from the Dean of Durham, the Very Revd W. C. Lake, dated 21 May 1878, of which I possess a copy, and in a testimonial from Dr Armes himself. The appointment is set down in West (see p xvi, n 1) as—Pupil of Dr Armes, and Assistant Organist at Durham Cathedral, Organist of St Oswald's, Durham 1876.

It emerges from the diary's pages that it was the duty of the senior apprentice to coach the younger apprentices in their studies in harmony, counterpoint, musical modulation, etc., and to supervise their daily work and practice in these subjects. So we find such entries in the diary as 'studied with Whitehead the first order of two-part counterpoint': (John Whitehead was the senior of the three apprentices): and, 'worked with John on our exercise in the third order of two-part counterpoint'. Of the next step, counterpoint in *three* parts, the diarist observes, 'It is very strict. I was about an hour and a half over one short exercise before I got it right'. Even when, in due course, 'the Doctor' (Dr Armes) took over personal tuition in these subjects, they, the apprentices, seem to have made it a rule, or a point of honour, to keep ahead of the Doctor in their work, so that when they went to him for a lesson they would have covered the ground already by themselves, and so might the better understand what he had to impart.

The day's work of the apprentices was a formidable one and started at a very early hour of the morning, after rising at five-thirty a.m. A typical time-table as set out in the diary, including attendance at the two daily services at the Cathedral (probably each of about one hour's duration) and daily choir practice, of say half an hour, shows a total of between ten and a half to eleven hours' work, not counting a quarter of an hour for lunch (!) and half an hour's walk. Nor was this all, for the evenings were spent by the three apprentices together in music-making with their master at his house. Dr Philip Armes conscientiously carried out as far as possible what he undertook in his apprentice's indenture, to instruct him 'in the highest branches of the Musical Art'. The means for this were modest compared to what they might be at the present day. In the music room of his home, he had, in addition to the pianoforte, a harmonium; one of the apprentices played the violin; and with these slender resources they endeavoured to explore systematically a substantial portion of the repertoire of music—chamber music, lieder, orchestral works and even opera. It must be observed however that the repertoire had its limitations and notable omissions. There is no mention in the diary of Chopin, of Schumann or of Brahms. Their studies of pianoforte music did not in fact go beyond the immediate successors of Beethoven, who had died no more than forty-four years before. These included Hummel, Czerny and Clementi—all minor composers as we would consider them now—though it did include the works of that later composer of stature, Mendelssohn. In their studies of opera, Wagner is not mentioned, though Weber is included.

Such general educational subjects as Latin and German (both entered in the day's timetable in the diary) had to be garnered by the apprentice if he chose to do so, under his own steam. My father, according to his own personal reminiscences, had acquired a smattering of Greek at the Duke's School before he left Alnwick; and his father, by correspondence or personal supervision on his occasional visits to see his son at Durham, was able to note progress and to guide him in such subjects.

The diary shows its writer to have possessed for his age a remarkable facility and swiftness in learning to play new and unfamiliar music. Thus we read that it took him no more than one day's practice probably amounting to about two hours, to master or 'almost master' one of Bach's forty-eight Preludes and Fugues. Those who have laboured to make the '48' their 'daily bread' as the saying is, may envy the speed of this accomplishment. He possessed the gift of absolute pitch to an extremely accurate degree, as I myself am able to confirm. Not only was he able to name the pitch of a note played on a musical instrument, but he could say in which of the various pitches then in use it lay, i.e. the low pitch of the organ, the medium pitch of the orchestra, or the old high pitch, now obsolete, of the instruments of the military band.

Outside the closed circle of the Cathedral and the other churches of Durham lay the secular musical activities of the city, which also find place in the diary—the Durham Musical Society, the Factory Choral Society, and such things as operetta, and vocal and instrumental concerts, in which the apprentices generally took part, by playing pianoforte accompaniments and solos.

Beyond these local activities again were the occasional expeditions outside the city's confines, to other towns within practical reach, such as Newcastle-upon-Tyne, to experience what must have been the ultimate musical revelation, of hearing recitals by great visiting artistes; for the day was yet far off and unimagined when it would be possible to hear the masterpieces of music in great and authoritative performance by the turning on of a switch on a radio set, or the spinning of a gramophone record on a turntable. The diary gives a vivid account of such a recital by the great pianist and conductor, Hans von Bulow; and of a visit further afield by another apprentice to hear Bach's Passion 'done by Hallé's Band'.

The oldest part of the city of Durham, is may be said, is almost an island. It takes the form of a narrow peninsula almost surrounded by the river Wear, except for an isthmus of little more than a quarter of a mile across. (In olden times the island conformation was completed by a moat cut across the isthmus for defensive purposes.) The perimeter of the city to the west and south is bounded by cliffs descending steeply to the river. The district lying across the river to the east, Elvet, is enclosed by a further curve of the river. It is a physical situation which seems from the account to have been reflected in a compact and close-knit quality of life in the city of the period somewhat akin to that of an actual island community. It is a quality that is reflected, albeit unconsciously, in the pages of the diary, adding palpably to its interest and quality.

Let it be said here however that the diary is not entirely taken up with music and with the diarist's daily studies, or with his playing the organ at the Cathedral or elsewhere in Durham. Incidents of personal concern and of the ordinary daily occurrences around him which catch his eye are captured on the wing and unfailingly set down in his pages; the local regatta, a visit to Durham of the Prince and Princess of Wales (later to become Edward VII and Queen Alexandra); a parliamentary election—in which with a knowledge of the world somewhat in advance of his years he suspects bribery!; a military review at Alnwick when he is home on a few days' leave; a vivid description of paper-chases in which he took part, and so on. These are interspersed with entries of a more personal nature, as the observation, early in the diary that 'we get good milk here,—*almost as good as in the country*!'; mention of visits by his father and mother; the rather touching accounts of broken chilblains on his fingers in the cold winter months; a bowel upset, suffered first by his master and then, immediately afterwards, by himself; the confession of having wasted his time by becoming engrossed in a book of tales of the Scottish/English Borders—an absorption with which all who have read these same tales will readily sympathise. . . .

The diary ends abruptly, to speak truth somewhat disconcertingly so, at the conclusion of his apprenticeship with the words, 'I go home on Monday morning.' The day was 9 August 1875. He was aged seventeen years, of which time his apprenticeship had occupied very nearly four years. In actual fact he was to return to Durham for a further two years of work and study, while he awaited the right appointment to come along, a time he was to put to good use, notably (in addition to his continued studies) as official organist of St Oswald's Church, following the death of Dr J. B. Dykes. On this further term the diary fails us; fortunately I have been able to complete the record from other sources. This I have set down in a final L'Envoi.

So now let *The Diary of an Organist's Apprentice* tell its own story.

To my dear wife, Elizabeth
Francis Collinson, 1982

THIS INDENTURE made the twenty-fifth day of September One thousand eight hundred and seventy-one *BETWEEN THOMAS COLLINSON* of Alnwick in the County of Northumberland and *THOMAS HENRY COLLINSON* son of the said Thomas Collinson of the one part and *PHILIP ARMES* of the City of Durham Esquire Doctor of Music and Organist of the Cathedral Church of Durham aforesaid of the other part . . .

WHEREAS the said Philip Armes has agreed with the said Thomas Collinson to take the said Thomas Henry Collinson his son as his Apprentice to be taught the profession of a Cathedral Organist Pianist and Composer of Music including the Art of Writing for an Orchestra and also in the highest branches of the Musical Art . . .

HE the said Thomas Collinson Doth Hereby Covenant with the said Philip Armes that he the said Thomas Henry Collinson shall and will diligently and faithfully serve the said Philip Armes as his apprentice for and during the said term as a faithful apprentice ought to do . . .

And the said Thomas Collinson . . . shall provide for the said Thomas Henry Collinson all manner of clothes, linen and other apparel fit and becoming for his use as apprentice to the said Philip Armes, and also with the washing and repairing thereof. . . .

THOMAS HENRY COLLINSON

DIARY

1871: Aged 13 [The diarist's age at the head of each page is an editorial addition]

October 5 Durham I arrived here at 11 o'clock a.m. and went to my lodgings which are very nice and comfortable. I had luncheon at Dr. Armes' and then wandered about until it was time for service (4 o'clock).[1]
After service I went into the school where the choristers had a practice. The weather has been fine with the exception of a little rain in the morning. The piano, to my surprise, was in good tune when I tried it.

6 Went to choir practice at half past eight a.m.—Service at ten o'clock. Saw mother off at two o'clock. Went back to Service at four. I had a piano lesson at the Doctor's[2] tonight, and have to work up Bach's first prelude and fugue[3] for next lesson. The weather has been very bright except at about 11 o'clock this morning when there was a rather heavy shower of rain.
My regular daily practice is to be two hours at the piano, and one hour at the organ.

7 Went with John Whitehead[4] into St. Nicholas' Church[5] and tried the organ, which is a very fine one. We then went through the market which is very large and was well attended today.
The organ in the Song-School is a very small weak instrument with only five stops and German pedals.[6] I have done some French tonight.
Whitehead has the Market Place Church[7] service all to himself now, and will begin his duties tomorrow morning. The choristers are a rough lot of boys.
I have almost mastered the first prelude and fugue in Bach. The organ music for the use of the apprentices is all found by the Cathedral.
Weather very fine to-day.

*8 **(Sunday)*** The whole peal of bells[8] in the Cathedral was rung today. It sounded very nice. Some of the churches have very good bells.

[1] Notes to Diary start on p 99.

Durham, Oct. 5th/71.

I arrived here at 11 o'clock a.m., & went to my lodgings which are very nice & comfortable. I had luncheon at Dr. Armes' & then wandered about until it was time for service (4 o'clock.) After service I went into the school where the chorister's had a practice. The weather has been fine with the exception of a little rain in the morning. The piano to my surprise was in good tune when I tried it.–

6th. Went to Choir Practice at half past eight a.m, Service at ten o'clock. Saw Mother off at 2 o'clock. Went back to Service at 4. I had ~~had~~ a piano lesson at the Doctor's to-night, & have to work up Bach's first prelude & fugue for next lesson. The weather has been very bright excep at about 11 o'clock this morning when there was a rather heavy shower of rain. My regular daily practice is to be two hours at the piano, & one hour at the organ

1. The first page of the Diary

1871, October: Aged 13

I went to St. Oswald's[9] tonight. Dr. Dykes played the organ. They have got a new Curate at this church. He read the prayers tonight. He was a chaplain in the navy.
I intend to go to St. Nicholas' next Sunday night.
The piano is in very good tune. It is in capital working order.
We had a pelting shower just before service this afternoon. I, fortunately, had my umbrella with me. I get very good milk here, just as good as in the country.
I got a letter from Mother last night, enclosing Richard's[10] and my own photograph.
I had a game at Besique the other night with Mr. Lawson;[11] he knows a little of the game. There is no practice after the Sunday afternoon service.
My watch keeps very correct time.

9 Very fine clear weather today. No rain. It was quite frosty tonight.
Dr. Armes set me some harmony to do for tomorrow morning. I have done most of it now.
The Dean[12] came into the Song-School when I was practising.[13] He asked me where I came from, and how I liked Durham. I can find my way about the streets quite easily now.

10 Quite frosty this morning. The fields were white with ryme. The day opened out into a very fine one.
Miss Henderson, daughter of the M.P. for Durham, was married today at St. Nicholas' church. John Whitehead played the Wedding March for them. The whole peal of bells in the Cathedral were set a-ringing for about an hour and a half.
I had two games of Besique with Mr. Lawson tonight in both of which I beat him. Turner's Diorama is in Durham just now. It is the same as that which visited Alnwick a year or two ago.

11 Nothing of importance today. I had two games of chess, one with Mr. Lawson, in which he gave in, and the other with his nephew who check-mated me.
Weather still fine.

13 I was not well today. I complained of dizziness and sickness. Took some magnesia which put me right. I strolled along to Nevil's Cross.[15] Nothing now is to be seen except an octagonal stone with a diminutive pillar fixed to it.

1871, October: Aged 13

14 Went through the Cathedral library.[16] It is very interesting. Saturday is one of the days on which the public can see it.
I went to the Doctor's tonight to get a harmony lesson. Whitehead was there at the same time.
I wrote home this afternoon. I expect an answer on Tuesday.
Came from the Cathedral by Prebends Bridge.[17] I therefore passed the Grammar School.
It is raining hard to-night.

15 ***(Sunday)*** Anthony Graham, one of Father's old scholars,[18] came to see me today. He was trying to find me out yesterday, but did not succeed.
Got a letter from Father. His letter crossed mine.
Went to St. Nicholas'. The service is simple.

16 The organ builder has been busy tuning the organ in the Cathedral. The weather is fine.

17 I had a piano lesson tonight. No. 2 Prelude and Fugue, Bach, and two more of Cramer's Studies[19] for next time.
There is a concert in the Town Hall got up by Lambert the music seller.

18 St. Luke's day. Wrote home this afternoon. Weather fine.

19 Gloomy weather. I had tea at Mr. Lambert's.

20 We had a great deal of rain last night, but it broke off into a very fine day today. The river was a good deal swollen.

21 I got an organ lesson after practice tonight on the Song School organ.

22 ***(Sunday)*** I went to St. Nicholas' again tonight, and sat in the organ loft. The church was crowded.
Weather fine. Went to Bear Park[20] to see the ruins there.

23 Nothing of importance today. Weather fine.

24 Weather very fine this afternoon.
I got all my practice in before dinner.[21] In the afternoon I wrote to Richard. After I had finished my letter I went to the Cathedral and had a game of football before service.
I went to the Doctor's tonight for a harmony lesson.

1871, October: Aged 13

25 I wrote home this afternoon. Did a French exercise tonight. Weather fair.

26 Weather rather damp and gloomy, but warm.

28 I went with one of the choir boys (W. Macbeth) up the Tower in the Cathedral. A splendid view can be obtained at the top. The staircase is very dark. St. Simon and St. Jude's day.

29 (Sunday) Weather fair. I went to tea at Mr. Gryce's.[22]

31 The weather is still pretty fair.

November 1 Weather fine. I wrote home today. All Saint's Day. There was organ in the afternoon as well as in the morning, a new rule having been made that if a Saint's day occurs on a Wednesday there is to be organ[23] in the afternoon. I had not time to answer any of the boy's [*sic*] letters.

3 I got leave for tomorrow, this morning.[24] It was readily granted.

10 I saw Mr. Thorpe of Ellingham in town. I could not speak to him as he was in company with another gentleman.
Weather rather frosty. It is Mayor's day today. The boys got a half holiday.

11 Got a letter from home tonight. I have been learning some German. Yesterday was the first day I had played a voluntary in the Cathedral.

12 (Sunday) I played the *in*-voluntary this morning.

13 Very frosty weather. The ground is quite hard.

15 Wrote home today. I went to hear the Service without the organ this afternoon. Whitehead was not at practice, he was unwell.

16 Went to St. Cuthbert's Church tonight. The river was frozen today.

26 (Sunday) Weather fair, rather damp. Got a letter from home last night.

1872, January: Aged 13

January 14 (Sunday) After my recent illness[1] I have ventured out as far as the Cathedral for the first time, the weather being dry.
I got a letter from home this morning enclosing twelve stamps and the French that I translated from "L'Histoire de Charles XII de Suede". I congratulate myself upon having done it very well.
It has been very lazy of me to neglect my diary for such a long time. However, I mean to make a point of writing something in this book every night. It is very useful so to do. Of course, I will not have much to put in, but I can just jot what music I have done through the day.
Great scarcity of ink. I joined Whitehead in the organ loft at St. Cuthbert's[2] this morning. I only went to the Cathedral in the afternoon. It was a great change to hear a bit of good music again.

15 I was at both morning and evening service today. The Doctor did not make his appearance. Martin[3] was in the organ loft this morning.
Done five hours piano practice. Not done much harmony tonight. Will do more tomorrow. Weather rather frosty. It softened in the afternoon.

16 Martin played a solo at Crossgate Readings[4] tonight. He was encored, and fully deserved the encore.

17 I did not go to church this morning as the air was too damp and drizzly. Wrote home.

18 Lent Whitehead the "Village Organist"[5] and Martin "Massaniello"[6] and "Zauberflote".[7]

19 Doctor not here in the morning.

20 Went up with Whitehead to St. Cuthbert's at 11 o'clock. Left all my organ music for Whitehead to use. Air frosty.
We had a beautiful anthem this afternoon—"As pants the hart".[8] It was sung very well. Nicholson sang the solo. He is getting on very well with his solo-singing. I like it better than Macbeth's.[9]
The men had no practice this morning. I know three of Webbe's Score Anthems.[10] I get on pretty well with them.
Martin is coming on Wednesday night to play the duets instead of tonight as he is engaged.

1872, January: Aged 13

22 The Doctor will be away all this week.

23 Went to Maclagan's mimic opera[11] in the Town Hall. It was very amusing.

24 Went to St. Cuthbert's Choir Practice. Played the duets with Martin.

25 Played duets for three hours all at one time with Martin. Lent Martin "Tarantella",[12] the duets and Heller.[13]

26 Did some harmony. Three hours and a half piano practice.

27 Done some Harmony and French. Played duets at Martin's this afternoon. Went with Whitehead to St. Cuthbert's.

28 I played in the morning. Went to St. Cuthbert's at night with Gryce.

29 Two hours organ practice. Played in morning. Learnt the sixth score anthem, Webbe. Done two French exercises and some harmony. Learnt a fugue in Rink[14] for tomorrow. Whitehead had to go to Dr. Armes' with his Bach and Cramer. I expect I will have to go some night this week.

31 Wrote home and sent some French and a kyrie[15] in G Minor. Dull weather in the morning, but fine in the afternoon. Went to hear the singing without organ.

February 1 Saw the two-headed Nightingale in the Cathedral, also the dwarf.[16] Had nearly two hours organ practice.

2 Done some harmony.

3 Did not play a voluntary.

4 Did not play a voluntary. Got a harmony lesson. The Doctor was pleased with the exercise done in advance. Had a practice at St. Cuthbert's. Went to the Training College for the parcel from Alnwick.[17]

5 Choral Communion this morning. Went to St. Cuthbert's, but did not sit in the organ loft.

6 Returned Webbe's anthems.

7 Had a piano lesson at 2 o'clock. Piano tuned by Mr. Young.

1872, February: Aged 13

8 Done some harmony.

9 No organ practice. Done some harmony.

10 Fine weather. Very short choir practice at night.

11 Went to St. Cuthbert's. Did not play. Afternoon anthem, "O Praise Jehovah's Goodness"—Beethoven.

12 Had a piano lesson. Played out evening.

13 Was with Whitehead in the library. He and I were at Dr. Armes' writing chants[18] from eight p.m. to a quarter past nine.

14 Wrote home.

15 Done some harmony.

16 Done some harmony.

17 Had a piano lesson.

18 *(Sunday)* Went to St. Cuthbert's.

21 Forgotten to write home. Piano lesson. Had to practice a sonata.

22 Wrote home instead of yesterday.

23 Saw Anthony Graham. He looked well. Very little piano practice.

24 Wrote a lot of Chants[19] for the Thanksgiving Day.

25 *(Sunday)* Went to St. Cuthbert's.

27 Thanksgiving Day. Upwards of 8000 people[20] in the Cathedral at morning service. The Dean preached.

28 Played at St. Cuthbert's Choir Practice, John Whitehead having to deputize for Dr Dykes. Piano lesson at four. Wrote home after tea.

29 Played a voluntary out of Rink.

1872, March: Aged 13

March 1 Got Heller back from Martin.

2 Harmony lesson with John Whitehead.

3 *(Sunday)* Got a letter from Father.

6 Played the Chants at Service.[21] First time. Played at St. Cuthbert's Choir Practice which is to be held in future in the Church.

7 Played out-voluntary evening, Fugue—Rink. University Sports. Done some harmony.

9 Harmony lesson.

11 Played out morning. Received a letter from W. Biggs [a former Alnwick schoolmate].

12 Had a short walk up Red Hills.[22]

15 Played at Dr. Armes' on his grand piano; John Whitehead on the harmonium. We had a cup of tea. Got Beethoven's Sonatas (Violoncello Part)[23] for next time.

16 Wrote to Fred, received a letter from him at night. Went with John Whitehead to St. Cuthbert's. T. W. Brewis[24] begun work at White's. Played out morning.

20 Wrote home. Played harmonium at Dr. Armes', John Whitehead the piano. Beethoven's Sonatas.

21 First Spring Day. Heavy fall of snow.

23 Got up early. Played the out-voluntary[25]; not very well tonight I am sorry to say.

24 *Palm Sunday.*

25 Played instead of John at the Factory Choral Practice.[26]

26 Wrote home.

27 Received an answer from home stating the time of Father's arrival tomorrow.

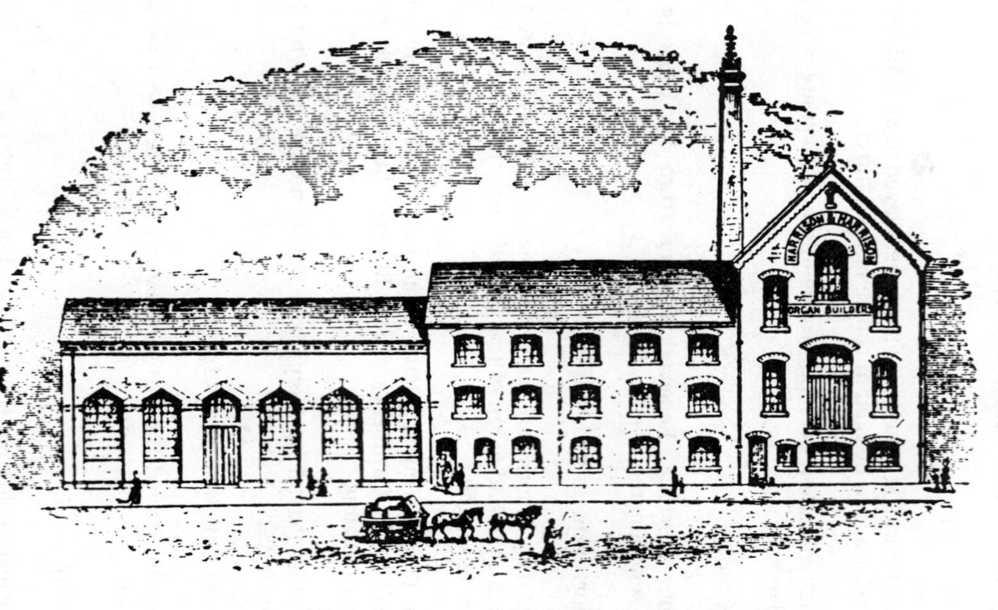

2. *The organ factory of Messrs Harrison & Harrison*

1872, March: Aged 13

28 Went at 2 o'clock to the Station, but Father did not come till 5.30.

29 ***Good Friday.*** Father went to St. Oswald's in the morning and the Cathedral in the afternoon.

30 Had a walk with Father and Mr. Lawson. Played out at evening service. Dr. Armes gave me leave from practice without my asking.

31 ***Easter Sunday.*** Father went with me to St. Cuthbert's in the evening. He and Mr. Whitehead made acquaintance with each other.

April 1 All Fools Day. Father went away at 3 o'clock in the afternoon. Did not go to the Cathedral on account of a cold and bad weather.

2 Made out a Routine of Work. In the house all day.

3 Went to Cathedral. Doctor gone away till Sunday.

4 They have begun scraping part of the nave.[27]

7 Dr. Armes came home. Went to St. Margaret's at night. Do not like the church. Mr. Robertson preached.

8 Fine weather. Dr. Armes has given me Mozart's Sonatas to learn, and Whitehead, Schubert's Sonatas.[28]

9 Very fine, warm weather. Practiced the "Son and Stranger"[29] duet. Learnt the nineteenth fugue, Bach.[30] Tried the next one, which is long and difficult.[31] Finished the Major Basses (Goss). Learnt "All Empires on God Depend" (Handel's Choruses).[32]

10 Rehearsal of the "Son and Stranger" at Atfield Hall. Took John's choir practice and played the interlude duet.

11 Played over the duet [from The Son and Stranger] to Dr. Armes. The operetta began at 8 p.m. Did pretty well.[33]

15 Went with Whitehead to Greatorex's[34] to be photographed with the performers.

16 Played chants over to Dr. Armes for St. Oswald's next Sunday.

1872, April: Aged 13

17 Took John's choir practice. Wrote home.

19 Attended service and choir practice at St. Oswald's. John played the service. St. Cuthbert's organ tuned.

20 Paid Mr. Lambert four shillings for piano tuning last February. Hiller tuned it in the afternoon. Paid him five shillings for it. Mr. Lawson got Vic, the dog, about two months old. Wet day. Sore eye. Got new trousers.

21 ***(Sunday)*** Played at St. Oswald's morning service, Dr. Dykes being away. Mr. Rogers preached and played there at night.

22 Mr. Lawson's birthday.

Aged 14

24 My birthday. Played the chants. Learnt the first part of Bach's fugues. Played at St. Oswald's.

25 Grammar School sports. No choir practice in the evening. Fine day. Done some harmony.

26 Rain. Copying "Holy Jesu"[35] into the new books. Played morning chants. Played at St. Oswald's.

27 Harmonized St. Oswald's "Nicene Creed"[36] for tomorrow morning. Harmony lesson. Wet weather. Played a nice fugue in A minor in the morning. Received a letter from home enclosing twelve stamps.

28 ***(Sunday)*** Played at St. Oswald's morning service. Choral Sacrament. Got on exceedingly well. Wet morning.

29 Done some harmony.

30 Done some harmony. Played at St. Oswald's.

May 1 Fine morning. Got up early. Played at St. Oswald's. I expect this is the last time.[37]

2 Played chants in the morning [in The Cathedral].

1872, May: Aged 14

3 Played chants in the morning. Wet day.

5 Played chants in Sunday morning service for the first time.

6 Played chants in the morning. Dr. Armes' anthem "I will sing a new Song", very good. Can manage King in F[38] pretty quick time from score. Learnt second fugue, Bach,[39] second part. Dull weather. Got up late. Mr. Greatorex's lecture on "Secular Music".[40] It was a very nice, interesting lecture. Far nicer than Dr. Dykes'. Not so positive and one-sided. Whitehead presided at the piano. Played the "Carman's Whistle"[41] and accompanied some songs, etc.

7 Saw Charles Morrell[42] in the Cloister. Promised to see him after service, but found he had gone away before I finished the out-voluntary. Got my hair cut.

8 Piano lesson—Mozart's Sonatas.

9 John had a piano lesson. Ascension Day. Long morning service. Had a short walk up Red Hills with John after morning service. Fine day.

10 Played chants morning and evening. The latter were difficult.

12 Dr. Armes sent me to St. Cuthbert's in the morning.

13 Played out, morning.

14 Played chants in the morning.

15 Played chants in the morning, one of which is the one for two trebles by Dr. Armes. It is a very good chant.

16 I will not put down when I play the chants in future now.

19 Went to St. Cuthbert's in the morning.

20 Whitsun Monday. Sports in Wharton's Park. Had a walk with T. W. Brewis and Vic to Bear Park. John away with his Father for a day's holiday.

25 Learnt 7th fugue, Bach, second part.[43]

1872, May: Aged 14

29 Royal Oak Day.[44] Went to the Palace Green to hear the singing from the top. It sounded very nice.

30 Learnt 8th fugue, Bach, part two.

June 1 Birth of Dr. Armes' son.

2 ***(Sunday)*** Went to St. Cuthbert's, morning and evening.

3 King in F today. Was not sung nicely. Boys kept in till six o'clock for it.

5 Wrote home. Posted the letter in the new post-box beside the Station. It is nearer than Crossgate pillar post.

6 I have put the "Swell to Great" coupler[45] wrong.

7 Dull, but not bad weather. Got up early. Short choir practice at night.

8 Was at Dr. Armes' playing Hummel's Sonatas[46] for piano and flute. They are difficult.

9 Went to St. Cuthbert's both morning and evening. Several very heavy storms of rain and some thunder.

10 Dull, wet weather. Some thunder. The summer weather is very backward this year.

11 Weather a little finer. St. Barnabas' Day. The junior boys, and one or two of the elder ones have to go to practice at 8.30 a.m. in future. The others, Whitehead and myself at 9 a.m. Piano duets, or piano and harmonium, I should say, at Dr. Armes'. John Whitehead and I.

12 The boys' trip to the Bishop's. Nice day. Dr. Armes gave John Whitehead and I holiday from afternoon service. We went with Malcolm to Finchale Abbey[47] by Kepier Wood[48] and came back by Framwellgate Moor.[49] Started off at two p.m. and came back at a little before eight. I enjoyed myself very much.
Got leave for a week's holiday.

1872, June: Aged 14

13 Wrote home. I ought to have written yesterday.

14 Piano lesson. Dr. Armes kindly told me that I might as well go away on Monday and stop till the last Saturday in June, which is about a fortnight. I will not be here at the Regatta,[50] but I do not care very much about that. I will be at home. Got up early this morning. Did two hours piano practice before morning choir practice. Done seven hours practice altogether.

15 Durham full of pitmen today. A meeting of the Durham Miners' Association. About twenty or thirty bands came with the men. The meeting was held on the racecourse. Written to Father to tell him that I am going home on Monday.

16 Went to St. Cuthbert's.

17 Went home. Train started at about five minutes to eleven. Had a bathe in the Brownie[51] and a long walk by Stone Bridge and Bear Park [Durham] before breakfast. Had a drive to Alnmouth [from Alnwick] and back in the afternoon. All well at home.

18 Had a practice on the organ in the church [St. Paul's Church, Alnwick].

20 The school-boys broke up for the holidays.

21 Went with St. Paul's choir picnic to Hulne Abbey.[53] A little rain in the evening. Militia Review today.[54]

22 Played for Mr. Moore at church today [at St. Paul's, Alnwick].

24 Played at church tonight. St. John the Baptist's Day.

26 Got up early and had a bathe at Alnmouth with W. Biggs.[56] Had breakfast at Wilson's of Lesbury.[57]

27 Went with Father, Mr. J. Hunter[58] and Fred to Howick[59] by Little Mill Station, and from there to Alnmouth by the shore. Nice day. Not too hot for walking. We started at half-past ten in the morning, and came back at seven p.m.

28 Packed up for tomorrow. Was at Thorpe's for tea.

1872, June: Aged 14

29 Arrived at Durham at half-past ten a.m. Started from Alnwick at twenty minutes to eight by slow train. Arrived at Newcastle at 9.45. Started for Durham from thence at 10 a.m. Fast train. Fare 4/5d.
Another six months work before me again. I hope I will use the time well. Dr. Armes gave me a lot of music tonight. Weber's Operas, Mozart's Variations, etc. It is very thoughtful of him. I cannot practice all the batch of music, but it will be getting a good stock in.

30 Went to St. Cuthbert's both morning and evening. Played out in the morning.

July 1 Dr. Armes gone away for his month's holiday.

2 A party of Civil Engineers from Newcastle at service this afternoon. Fine weather.

3 Got up early and did some writing for the St. Cuthbert's choir.

4 Hot day. Had some duet playing with John at his house.

5 Hot day.

6 Got up early and did some more writing. Began at 3.30 a.m.

7 Played at St. Cuthbert's in the morning. John at the Cathedral. We both got on very well.

8 Done a lot of writing this morning. I shall soon have it finished.

9 Finished the chant writing.

10 Wrote home. Went to St. Cuthbert's Choir Practice.

11 Got up late. Mr. S. Reay[60] at the Cathedral. Wet day. No practice at night.

13 Wet weather. Had some duets with John at Dr. Armes'.

14 Got on very well indeed at St. Cuthbert's. Mr. Reay at the Cathedral.

16 No practice tonight. Had a game with John Whitehead in the hay on Red Hills.

1872, July: Aged 14

17 No practice at all today. The schools are being whitewashed and cleaned.

18 The schools look very nice indeed. Got the loan of Whitehead's blue Bach to copy the last prelude and fugue from.

19 Got up early. Done the Bach copying. Stitched it into the book. Returned Whitehead's copy.

20 Hot weather. Got up late. They have begun putting stained glass in the windows of the Nine Altars.[61]

21 Played at St. Cuthbert's in the morning.

22 Got up early and had a bathe. Piano duets with John Whitehead at Dr. Armes'.

23 Duets.

24 Duets from 2 p.m. to 5 p.m.

25 Duets. Mr. Lawson gone to Barnardcastle. A niece of his here.

26 Got up early. Fine morning.

27 Whitehead been putting one of the notes of the Song-School organ right.

28 Played at St. Cuthbert's. We expected Dr. Armes at home this morning, but he has not come. Went to St. Oswald's tonight.

August 4 Whitehead gone to St. Cuthbert's again. Dr. Armes gave us some more music last night. I got Weber's piano and violin sonatas, Schubert's piano and violin sonatas, Haydn's piano and violin sonatas and Mozart's pieces.

6 Dr. Armes gone away for a day or two. Transfig Day.

7 Very nice weather.

3. St Cuthbert's Church, Durham

1872, August: Aged 14

8 Boys' trip to Tynemouth. John Whitehead and I went after morning service. We had a bathe, a row and all sorts of amusement. Nice tea. Went from Newcastle by steamboat. Dr. Armes here.

9 Weather fine, not hot.

10 Weekly rehearsals recommenced. Piano lesson. New Bach.

11 Played out-voluntary in the morning. Went to St. Cuthbert's at night.

12 Got up early. Rather cold.

13 Have not to go to morning practice till 9.15 a.m. until further orders. Saturday morning excepted.

14 Written a few lines to Sam in my letter home.

15 Weather fine.

16 Harmony lesson with John at Dr. Armes'.

17 They have taken the partition[62] down at the Cathedral to put it higher up the Nave. Duets with Dr. Armes. (Piano and violin.)

18 Hot day. Went to St. Oswald's in the evening.

19 Written to Father. His birthday.

20 Weather fair. I am on at present with the melodies in Goss.[63] Heard from Sam.

21 Weather fair. Went with the Music-boys to Dr. Armes' after practice.

22 Weather fair. The boys are trying some new services by Garret, M.D.[64]

23 Fine weather. Played at St. Oswald's. Had a practice afterwards for Sunday. T.W.B. completed his first trial week at Wesleyan School.

24 Nicholson[65] came back after a fortnight's holiday. Dr. Armes is not very well just now I think. He has been complaining of diarrhoea. St. Bartholomew.

1872, August: Aged 14

25 Played at St. Oswald's, morning and evening. Choral Sacrament in the morning. Wet day.

26 Rifle Review at Lampton.[66] Not well. Diarrhoea.

27 John and I went to Redcar with St. Margaret's and St. Cuthbert's choirs by the cheap trip. Started off about 7 a.m. I was, from twelve o'clock very bad indeed with the diarrhoea. It was perfect misery. I walked with great pain. We had dinner at 2 p.m., and tea at 5 p.m. Got home at about 10.15 p.m. Fine weather.

28 A good deal better today. Weather fair, not warm. Received a parcel from Mother, by Miss Stewart, containing 5s, a new shirt, two pairs of woollen socks and a pair of drawers.

29 Duets with John at Dr. Armes'.

30 Slight showers of rain at intervals. They will do no harm though. It is not what can be called a disagreeable day. It is very nice to-night. The nights of summer are the most delightful parts I think. Everything seems so calm. I should think the trip season will soon be over. What quantities there have been. Trips to Durham seem always to be well patronized.

31 Last day of August. The months soon slip away. John is not well today. Some rain.

September 1 Damp weather. Played at the time of communication [i.e. Communion] at the Cathedral. Went to St. Cuthbert's at night.

2 Weather fair. Dr. Armes' anthem this afternoon, "I Will Sing".

3 Good deal of rain. Autumn will soon be coming on. I observed a good many fallen leaves on the Broken Wall Walk.[67] Was to have had my organ practice this afternoon, but was deterred from having it by Dr. Armes giving a lesson. Done some extra harmony instead. Getting on nicely with the Melodies. The boys, I hear, have had an invitation to go to Canon Eade's for tea at 6 o'clock tomorrow night. I should think Mr. Hiller will come to the piano tomorrow.
The days are getting a great deal shorter now. It is dusk at about seven. There is some Rifle Competition going on at Kepier. Dr. Armes was away from church today. I think it was to go to the shooting. Good deal of beautiful blue lightning tonight, no thunder.

1872, September: Aged 14

4 Schoolboy's flower show at home today. Got no organ practice except about ten minutes, on account of Miss Greatorex[68] coming to practice.

5 Piano duets with John Whitehead at Dr. Armes'. Mozart's Quartettes. Alnwick Flower Show today.

6 Went to St. Oswald's tonight. Dr. Dykes played at service. I had a practice with the choir afterwards, Dr. Dykes presiding. Agricultural Show at Durham today.

7 Was with John in the organ loft from 11 a.m. to 1.30 p.m., putting some notes right.[69] Weather fair.

8 Played at St. Oswald's morning and evening. Played out-voluntary in the afternoon at the Cathedral for the first time. Played a fugue in D minor, Hesse.[70] Weather fair. Little damp.

10 Mr. Hiller tuned the piano today. Finished Goss' Melody Chapter. Damp weather.

11 Fine day. Played at St. Cuthbert's choir practice for Sunday. Strong wind tonight. Written to Mr. Crament.[71] Have not sent the letter off yet. Got St. Cuthbert's keys in my charge.

12 John gone with his Father into Yorkshire and Lancashire for a fortnight. Nice morning. Boys have been playing with the new football Canon Eade gave them.

13 Took the morning service. Nobody in the organ loft with me. This is the first time. Ouseley in Eb,[72] "Is it nothing to you"—Ouseley.[73] Did all except the anthem in the afternoon. Nice weather.

14 Tried Little Bow Church organ.[74] It is small.

15 Nice day. Played at St. Cuthbert's, morning and evening. Played out-voluntary in the afternoon. "O Love Divine"—Handel.

16 Weather fair, not fine. Written to John. Taken St. Cuthbert's organ keys to Mr. Donkins. Piano lesson. Yellow Back [i.e. music book with yellow-backed cover] and duets from Mozart's instrumental works.

17 Weather fair. Copied "A" Te Deum chants into the boys' church chant books.

1872, September: Aged 14

18 Heard from John. Sent him Smart's Organ Student[75] and Stone's[76] arrangements. Nice day. Wind rather strong.

19 Found out that I have forgotten to go to St. Cuthbert's choir practice last night. They had a practice without the organ. Weather rather cold. Went to Dr. Armes' to play some duets, but was set on with Mendelssohn's Songs without Words instead as the Dr. did not come to me till about a quarter to nine. Wet night. Copied the "B" Te Deum Chants into the boys' church chant books.

20 Weather cold, I think a little frosty. Took the morning service. Chant Te Deum and Jubilate,[77] and "The Lord will deliver"—Greene.[78] In the afternoon I started my piano practice as usual, but went on playing till five minutes to four, not looking at my watch till then; I ran all the way to the Cathedral, got there about two minutes after four. I felt quite sore for some time after. The Doctor was displeased with my being late. He was just in time himself, I imagine. It was my place to be there in time. He generally trusts to us being there so that he need not hurry.

21 St. Matthew. Had some practice on St. Cuthbert's organ in afternoon. Nicholson[79] blew for me. Very cold and dry.

22 Played at St. Cuthbert's. Played one of Mendelssohn's Leiders 4 Bk 1 and "We Never Will Bow Down"—Handel, as voluntaries in the evening. Played out-voluntary in the afternoon. One of Czerny's pieces.[80]

23 Damp and cold. Had an anthem in the afternoon which I have not heard in the Cathedral before, "Comfort Ye My People"—Handel.[81]

24 Damp and cold. When I was sitting in the kitchen with my harmony, Wortley[82] came with a message from his father asking me to go immediately to the Free Masons' Hall to play. I went (nine p.m.) and had to accompany the songs. It was an easy job, just sitting at the piano playing, and having what I like to eat and drink. I had Sherry, Brandy and all sorts of things offered to me. Afterwards the gentlemen clubbed together and gave me 10/10d. I got home about 1.15 a.m.

25 Terribly strong wind and much rain. Took the morning service—Rogers in D[83] and "O Pray For The Peace"—Purcell.[84] Played Rogers in D from the large Boyce[85] score. Went to St. Cuthbert's practice.

26 Nice day. Whitehead not come back yet.

1872, September: Aged 14

27 Took the morning service. Chants and "Call To Remembrance" Farrant.[86] Piano lesson. Bach's 48.

28 Father come to Durham. Came about half-past three p.m. Did not expect him then. Got a new-bound psalter for the Organ Loft and a few for the boys. John came home.

29 Father and I ate dinner at Dr. Armes'. He and I went to St. Cuthbert's at night. St. Michael and All Angels.

30 Fine day. Father had to go away in the morning for fear the Duchess[87] wanted him. Paid Mr. Lawson up to last Saturday.

October 1 Several of the Durham drapers begin today closing early in the winter months. Fair weather. Piano duets with John at Dr. Armes'. Mozart.

2 Went to St. Cuthbert's practice. Lent John my Heller.

3 Piano duets with John at his house. Got the loan of Dussek's Sonatas[88] Vol. 1 from John.

4 Nice day. Duets with John at his house. We are learning a concert piece by Dussek, and "Nocturne" by Hummel.

5 Cold, sharp weather. Duets with John at Dr. Armes'—Mozart.

6 Nice day, rather cold. Played at St. Cuthbert's, morning. Dr. Armes away today. We expect he will stay away for a few days.

7 Wet morning. Wet all day.

8 Very nice day. I took a holiday between 11 a.m. and 4 p.m. I took Vic, the dog, to the Brownie Stakes for a wash before dinner and went with John by Western Hill way to Bear Park. We got plenty of brambles,[89] such as they were. They had no flavour and were neither sweet nor sour. Duets at night with John at his house. We played from some of Dr. Armes' music, Bach, Mozart, Schubert. Whitehead has lent me a Prelude and Fugue by Mendelssohn. He played one of Mr. Rowton's cradle songs to me. It was a charming thing.[90]

9 Tried the Mendelssohn Prelude and Fugue.[91] It is perfection. Fine day.

1872, October: Aged 14

10 Very wet day. Dr. Armes came home last night at midnight. He was not at the Cathedral today.

11 Dr. Armes here in the afternoon. Cold day. Duets with John on his piano. Put 5/- into the bank, and sent my bank-book to the General Post Office Savings Bank Department yesterday. Got Cherubini.[92]

12 Cold day. My chilblains are beginning on my hands. John was at Mr. Lawson's before dinner, studying Cherubini with me. Went with him to a concert in the Town Hall at 2 p.m. Mr. D. Lambert invited us. It was a very good concert. Small audience. The artistes were—Madame Patey, Miss Edith Wynne, Mr. Patey and Mr. Arthur Byron. Accompanist—Mr. Stanislaus. The new shoes came for the boys to wear in church. Lent John my large book of modern pieces and the gavottes. He lent me, last night, three Beethoven's Sonatas and a fugue by Mendelssohn.

13 Went with John to St. Cuthbert's in the morning. Nice day, with the exception of a heavy shower at 8 p.m.

14 Foggy weather. University started again. I have been trying one of Beethoven's Sonatas (No. 7 in D)[93] which Whitehead lent me. It is a fine sonata. The Largo part is very fine.

15 Foggy weather. Frosty. The morning mail was an hour late through the foggy air. Harmony lesson with John at Dr. Armes'. Begun the Minor Basses.

16 Fair weather. Studied Cherubini with John at 4 p.m. in the School. We were to go to Dr. Armes' at night to have some duets, but Whitehead had to go to St. Cuthbert's Practice.

17 Fair weather. Harvest Thanksgiving at St. Oswald's.

18 Fair weather. I made a mistake in playing the evening psalms. I began with the wrong chant which was in a different key to the right one. St. Luke. Prince and Princess of Wales are coming past Durham about eleven tonight. They have been staying at Chillingham.[94]

19 The Prince and Princess[95] did not come past Durham till after twelve p.m. They came by a regular train, not a special. Mr. Walker and D. Lambert raised the tune of "God Bless the Prince of Wales". John was at the station. He got close to the Prince. (The train stopped in the station.) Fair weather today. Studied Cherubini with John at his place this morning.

1872, October: Aged 14

20 Harvest Festival at St. Cuthbert's. Nice day. The Principal of the Training College officiated at St. Cuthbert's in the morning.

21 Wet weather.

22 Fair weather. An accordian [*sic*] and a violin played together, sound very nice. There were two men playing them in the streets this morning. Went to Bear Park for my fortnightly ramble. Took Vic with me. John would not go. I enjoyed the walk very much indeed, and felt a great deal better for it. Duets with John at Dr. Armes'.

23 Studied Cherubini and Goss with John in school at 4 p.m. Fair weather. Piano practice—3½ hours, Organ—0, Harmony—2¼ hours.

24 Weather rather damp. Roads muddy. Went with Martin, his father and Mr. Price to Ushaw College.[96] Started after morning service. I saw over the College Museum. It is a rich collection of all kinds of curiosities. The stuffed birds were splendid. There was an alligator, and two young crocodiles; Chinese things; Indian Statuettes in wax representing the various costumes, etc.; valuable shells, old coins, and thousands of valuable things. The birds were the greatest feature. I tried the organ. It is an old one, built by Bishop. Three manuals. About 26 stops. I liked the Open Diapason. The full swell was very good. It has a double.[97] When we came away, the porter, who was very kind and obliging, told me to come again some finer day and he would show me all over. I had only seen a part of the College. We had dinner coming back, at an Inn on the roadside.
Piano practice—2 hours, Organ, Theory—1 hour. St. Margaret's School lectures began tonight.

25 Heavy showers at 5.30 p.m. I did not put a top-coat on this afternoon so got wet. The boys are learning a new service. Garrett in F.[98] Duets with John at Dr. Armes'. Piano practice—2¾ hours, Organ—2 hours, Theory—1½ hours.

26 Weather damp. Sometimes a little rain. Went with John at 8 p.m. to the Castle Choral Union Practice.[99]
Piano practice—3 hours, Organ 0, Theory—2 hours.

1872, October: Aged 14

27 On account of the Cathedral service on Sunday mornings being at 10.30 a.m. instead of 10 a.m., Dr. Armes has arranged to do without a Sunday morning practice. I have to be there at 10.15 a.m. to see to the books, etc. being all right.
Whitehead has not come at all in the morning. He will just go straight to St. Cuthbert's. Fair weather.

28 Fine day, especially the afternoon. John had his organ practice before dinner. St. Simon and St. Jude. John gone with his mother to Newcastle to hear one of Mr. Rae's[100] concerts.
Piano practice—3¼ hours, Organ—1¼ hours, Theory—1¼ hours.

29 Fair weather, windy night. Dr. Armes played Boyce in G from the treble copy, this morning's service. Harmony lesson with John at Dr. Armes'. Begun sequence basses.
Piano practice—2½ hours, Organ—2 hours, Theory (besides the lesson)—1 hour.

30 Went to Newcastle at 8.30 a.m. to spend the day with Father and Mother. I had to wait for them till 11 a.m. They came by a trip. They both looked well. We went to the Art Gallery which contained a large collection of pictures, stuffed birds, etc. Mother got her photograph taken at Downey's. We had tea there. Got a new hat, 4/6d. Mrs. Downey kindly invited me to call on them on my way home at Christmas. She got my Durham address so that she might send me some photographs some time. Father and Mother left Newcastle at 6 p.m. There was no train my way till 7.30 p.m. Father would not let me stop to the Town Hall Concert. (Mr. Rea's)

31 Fine day. Practiced Massaniello, Auber: and Nocturne, Hummel, with John at his place for an hour. He had to go to the Castle[101] at 8 p.m. to have a practice with the Students.[102]
Piano practice—2 hours, Organ—2 hours. (Lessons or duet-playing or anything of that sort not counted in the day's list of work done). Received a packet of photographs from Mrs. Downey. (Twenty)

November 1 Fair weather. Given John some photographs with which he was much pleased. Sent a letter of thanks to Mrs. Downey. "All Saint's [*sic*] Day." We had not the chants to play for this morning, they were at Dr. Armes'. John had to play them off a treble copy. Nearly two hours duet-playing with John at his place. We intend playing Massaniello and Nocturne tomorrow night [i.e. at the Castle concert]. Piano practice—1½ hours, Organ—1 hour.

1872, November: Aged 14

2 Cold weather. Practiced Garrett in F and "Jesu, King of Glory"—Bach, at the rehearsal. Dr. Armes had difficulty in pulling them along in Garrett in F, they dragged behind so. I have put off writing in here till Monday 4th, so I have forgotten how much work was done today. Played Massaniello and Nocturne with John at the Castle. The concert went off very nicely. The piano was not up to much. Duets with John on my piano.

3 Choral Sacrament this morning. Did not get out till 1.05 p.m. Nicholson went with me to St. Cuthbert's at night. We had arranged to go together to St. Margaret's, but I remembered that I had left my prayer-book at St. Cuthbert's. I got it again. It was in the same seat. Fine day.

4 Rose at 7.30 a.m. Cold weather. John had to write four or five treble copies of "I have surely built thee"—Boyce. He would not let me help him.
Piano practice—3¼ hours, Organ—1 hour, Theory—1 hour.

5 Rose at 7 a.m. Very nice, sunny day. This is Guy Fawke's Day. I remember last year at this time Father had just finished his visit here. Piano practice—4 hours, Organ—1¾ hours, Theory—1 hour.

6 Rose at 7.10 a.m. Fine day. Terribly windy. It is fearful tonight. I could hardly keep my feet. I lost my every-day hat at the bottom of Sutton Street under the Viaduct. I had to go to St. Cuthbert's in the dark to get the organ books for the practice at the Mission Rooms. The church is being painted. John and I went to Dr. Armes' at 2.15 p.m. to copy "Sing to Jehovah" Graun,[103] but Dr. Armes had not set us a copy so we went on with duets (Mozart) instead for two hours. John gone to Hetton[104] Concert with some of the men tonight. I had to give the music-boys their lessons after practice. Did not get home till seven. I had five boys to look over. Played at John's choir practice. Piano practice—2 hours, Organ— , Theory—1 hour.

7 Rose at 8 a.m. Fine day. Wind not quite so strong as last night. It blew some chimney-pots down. John and I written a copy each (treble) of "Sing to Jehovah"—Graun. Piano practice—3 hours (all at once tonight), Organ—1½ hours, Theory—1 hour.

8 Rose at 7.50 a.m. Fine day. The boys were invited by Mr. Lambert to go to his concert in the Town Hall. (The Tyrolese Concertos). Duets with John at Dr. Armes' (Beethoven). Piano practice—3 hours, Organ—1½ hours, Theory—1 hour.

1872, November: Aged 14

9 Nice day. One hour's harmony and one hour's duet-playing with John here this afternoon. Piano practice—1½ hours, Theory—nothing besides the lesson with John.

1872	SPENDINGS	
July 1st	One lead pencil	1d.
July 13th	Piece of drawing paper	1½d.
July 14th	Bag of Filberts	1d.
July 17th	Music paper for completion of Bach	4d.
August 27th	Toll at Redcar Pier Gate	1d.
August 30th	1 quire of Music Paper	1/6d.
September 2nd	Hair cut	3d.
September 16th	Piano tuning—Hiller	5/-d.
September 25th	Fees for use of Practice Organ	2/-d.
October 4th	Prayer Book for Baxter	1/-d.
October 4th	One lead pencil	1d.
October 4th	Two quill pens	1d.
October 7th	[left blank]	1d.
October 8th	Pears	2d.
October 10th	Boots Soled	3/9d.
October 14th	Note Book	6d.
October 21st	Apples	1d.
October 30th	Fare to Newcastle	2/3d.
October 30th	"Newcastle Magazine"	1d.
November 9th	Cocoanut	6d.

1872, November: Aged 14

10 Canon Evans preached a very eloquent sermon this morning. I went to St. Cuthbert's at night. Very cold weather.

11 Weather very cold. Rose at 7.30 a.m. John and I each did another copy of "Sing to Jehovah"—Graun. We only have one more copy to do now. We did one on Saturday morning. Wet night. Piano practice—3 hours, Organ—1¼ hours, Theory—1 hour.

12 Rose at 8.30 a.m. Wet day. The afternoon was fair. Harmony lesson with John at Dr. Armes'. Piano practice—2 hours, Organ—2 hours, Theory—1¼ hours.

13 Rose at 8.15 a.m. Damp, cold day. Occasionally a little snow, sometimes hail. Studied with John at the Song-School. Fourth order of two-part counterpoint,[105] and an exercise in the Third order upon an original subject for Saturday. Written a long letter home this afternoon. 3½ sheets. Received a letter of 8 sheets from Robert for John this morning. Mrs. Lawson guessed the secret that the Manchester letters are for John through me. Piano practice—1¼ hours.

14 Rose at 8.45 a.m. Cold, damp, heavy day. Have a very bad cough. Did not go to the Cathedral this afternoon. Dr. Armes very kindly sent word by Gryce at night that I was to stay away and nurse myself until the cold gets better. Mr. Bainbridge, Solicitor, Middlesbro', nephew of Mr. Lawson, here for tea. Piano practice—3½ hours, Organ—1½ hours.

15 The cold is accompanied by sickness and headache. Nicholson came up at 12 with a note from John telling me that the Doctor had promised Mr. Wray that I should play for him on Sunday. John was to go to the practice tonight.

16 Sickness and headache very bad. John came up in the afternoon. We did not play any duets. Could not go to the Castle Concert tonight. John played two solos instead of the duets. He was encored.

17 Mrs. Lawson would not let me go to St. Oswald's. They have got a Training Student to play for them. Feel rather better.

18 Received a railway parcel from Father containing a Mackintosh with a note which I answered at night.

20 Went to the Cathedral. Dr. Armes kindly told me to stop at home till the end of the week to nurse my cough.

1872, November: Aged 14

21 Had a short walk at noon. T.W.B. taken ill.

22 Damp day.

23 T.W.B. has the Scarlet Fever.

24 Canon Evans preached a nice sermon upon the Lord's Prayer. Fair weather. Mr. T. Rogers is Precentor now. This is his first Sunday. Music—Dykes in F, "O Saviour of the World"—Goss; Dykes in F, "Glory, Honour"—Mozart. I am advised by Dr. Jepson to quit Mr. Lawson's till T.W.B. is better. Mr. Lawson has taken me to Mrs. Dalby's to stop.

December 13 Left Mrs. Dalby's. During the time I have been there I have been three times to play duets at Dr. Armes'. The Judges came to the Cathedral on Wednesday morning (11th Dec.). Went to the last Castle Concert of the present term last Saturday night. Received 10/- for going there to play duets. Last night, after service, Dr. Armes came to me to say that if I wanted any holiday I was to go as soon as I liked, to come back two days after Christmas Day. The weekly bills of music to be performed are printed now. Gone home by the Express Train which stops here at 4.30 p.m. Father and Mother, and all well.

18 School examination [at Alnwick]. Mr. Rushton, Diocesan Inspector, examined.

22 Played at St. Paul's [Alnwick] for Mr. Moore.

24 Went with the choir to the Castle [Alnwick] for the Carol Singing. They sang round the town afterwards, but I was asleep.

25 Christmas Day. They had two anthems at the Church. Pergolesi's[106] Gloria and Mozart's Gloria. They spoiled the latter.

26 Went with Sam to Ambul [*sic. recte* Amble]. Walked round with Mr. Henderson, Adam Scott[107] and Sam to Alnmouth where we saw the pieces of wreck which had been washed up.

27 Came back to Durham. Started from Alnwick at 12.20 p.m. Had to wait about half an hour at Bilton. Got to Durham at 3 p.m. Express train.

30 Dr. Armes gone away.

1872, December: Aged 14

31 Had a practice on St. Cuthbert's organ. Scott kindly offered to blow for me.

1873

January 1 T.W.B. woke me at midnight to hear the bells ring in the New Year.[1] Mother would get my letter this morning. I received one from Father, a very nice letter full of good advice, which with God's help, I will try to follow.

12 Played at St. Cuthbert's this, and last Sunday morning. Hallelujah Chorus (Handel) this afternoon.

Went with John, Brotherton and another young man up the Tower. We saw the bells. We went along where they light the gas and along to one of the Western Towers.

15 Harmony and Counterpoint with John at the Song-School. For next time—Finish Modulation,[2] and an exercise in every order we have learnt.

16 Whitehead not well tonight. He was at Mr. Roger's last night. I took his practice for him. I am learning Latin.

18 Mr. Rogers came into the organ-loft this afternoon. He played the Psalms. He spoilt them. The singers laughed at him. Duets with John at night. Counterpoint for next time—exercise in each order except the first. Harmony—Modulation Exercises.

19 Played at St. Cuthbert's this morning. Mr. Ridley gave orders for the Psalms to be chanted as the Venite is part of the morning's Psalms. They were done very well.

20 Fall of snow last night, two inches thick. Frosty this afternoon. The roads are very slippery.

21 Took the dog a walk round by Raleigh Paper Mill before dinner. Fine anthem this afternoon—"We Praise Thee O God"—Purcell. It was to have been Handel, but was changed.

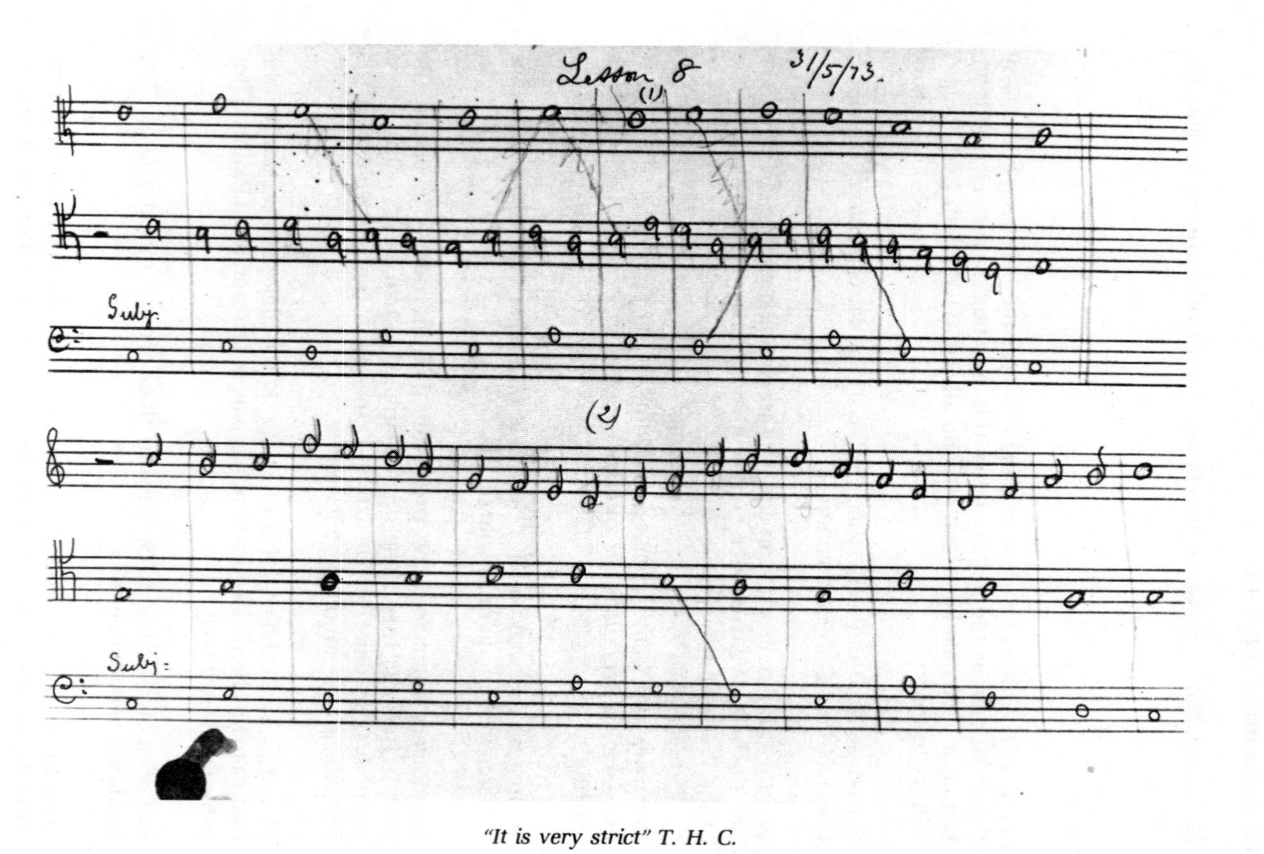

"It is very strict" T. H. C.

4. Counterpoint exercise, second order in three parts

1873, January: Aged 14

22 Snow melting away fast. Dr. Dykes wants me to play at his church on Sunday morning, but I am afraid it cannot be done as I have to go to St. Cuthbert's.

23 Dr. Dykes is going to ask Mr. Ridley permission to let Martin go to St. Cuthbert's on Sunday morning.

24 Mr. Ridley has given leave for Martin playing at St. Cuthbert's. I went to St. Oswald's service and played at Choir Practice tonight.

25 Written out a list of tomorrow morning's work at St. Cuthbert's for Martin. Frosty weather. Great many people went yesterday and today to a pond at Offal to skate.

26 Played at St. Oswald's morning. Choral Communion. The Dr. has written out a list for me.

27 Damp weather. Went to Whitehead's for tea. Studied harmony, and counterpoint alongside of John and played some duets with him. (Mozart's Symphonies and "Reformation Symphony"—Mendelssohn.)

28 Frosty morning. The chilblains on my hands are getting better. They have been very bad.

29 Written to cousin Richard. His birthday was yesterday, but I forgot about it till reading Mother's letter again today. He is 25 years of age.

30 Dr. Armes was at both services today. He is very pleasant. He has brought me the Second [book] of Bach.

31 Played Wesley in F (recit:)[3] this morning. Dr. Armes has given me leave from evening practice, and Whitehead from morning practice.

February 1 Harmony and counterpoint with John at his house. We are doing the second order of three-part counterpoint. It is very strict. I was about an hour and a half over one short exercise before I got it right. Dr. Armes played the anthem "Glory, Honour"—Mozart very well indeed this afternoon. I have never seen him play it better. Received £1.5s. and a parcel containing—Colenso's Arithmetic—January number of "Musical Monthly"—some music paper and two nightshirts, by Mr. Douglass of the Training College, from home. A letter from W. Biggs enclosed in Mother's letter.

1873, February: Aged 14

2 Snow.

3 A deal of snow. Duet practice at John's for next Saturday night. Took two organ pipes, Alto and Treble C, choir open diap., in a box to the station for Gray and Davidson,[4] London.

4 Snow melting fast. Went to Dr. Armes' after evening service with Whitehead to write out a treble of "Saviour of Men". (Taken from Haydn's—Seven Last Words From The Cross.) Saw Mr. J. Marshall[5] and his bride after morning service. They both looked well.

5 A lot of writing this afternoon, nearly four hours. No harmony lesson.

6 John and I did a bass copy each of the new Haydn anthem before dinner. The chilblains on my hands are troublesome. The broken one is not healed yet.

7 Played Tallis in D[6] from the Boyce score at morning service. Music writing before and after dinner.

8 Harmony and Counterpoint with John before dinner. After, duets. He has got some of Mozart's string pieces as piano duets. Castle Concert. Played two duets, the second of which was encored—Sonata—Beethoven, and part of a Mozart Symphony. Mrs. Whitehead has kindly given me a lotion for my chilblains.

9 Went to Dr. Armes' after church to-night to play some of Handel's oratorio choruses.

10 Played Child in G, morning.

11 Whitehead gone to Sedgefield for two days. I went to the first meeting of the Durham Musical Society[7] to-night, in the Assembly Rooms. The Dean made a short speech before business began, and after it was finished they did two or three of Mendelssohn's part-songs and a chorus out of Solomon—Handel.

12 Dull, heavy weather. Took morning service—Kempton in B^b, and "Not Unto Us", Walmisley.[8] No lesson with John as he is away. Played at St. Cuthbert's choir practice.

1873, February: Aged 14

13 John has come back.

14 Valentine Day. Little Charlie Mattison sent me one. A new anthem this afternoon—"Saviour of Men" adapted to the first of Haydn's "Seven Last Words From The Cross". Harmony lesson with John at Dr. Armes'.

15 Counterpoint with John before dinner. Duets here after. Very nice day.

16 Parts of Mozart's twelfth Mass[9] for the anthem this afternoon, viz.—Qui Tollis, Kyrie Eleison and Gloria. Mother says in her letter that Fred[10] received a take-off Valentine—a lad in shirt sleeves pounding at a mortar, and on his back written "Black Draught 6d.". Sam[11] got one from—yes I know whom.

17 Frosty weather. I have 14 chilblains on my hands. Two are broken, the flesh is quite raw and the sores have enlarged all round the sticking plaster. Harmony lesson with John at Dr. Armes'.

18 Mrs. Lawson has put some salve on my fingers. Went with John to Dr. Armes' and had some score-reading and part of one of Beethoven's String Trios arranged for piano duets.

19 They are putting up a raised flooring of wood for the altar in the nave.

21 John's first finger of the right hand is gathering. A new morning and evening service in D and F by Dr. Arnold[12] of Winchester done for the first time.

22 Counterpoint and Harmony with John. He went to the Castle by himself tonight. I went along with the confirmation boys to Mr. Roger's[13] at 6.30 p.m. I played two duets with him, Mozart duet and Haydn Symphony, on his grand piano. We had a few games at cards at the end of which we each received a little memento. I got a snuff-box. We then had supper and Mr. Rogers got out a lot of photographs of places on the Continent, the Alps, etc., and told us what he knew about them. He told us about St. Ambrose's Church in Milan, that it was built in the fourth century.

23 Slight fall of snow accompanied with frost.

24 Very frosty.

1873, February: Aged 14

25 A few inches of snow on the ground. The river is bearing in some parts, but it is not safe enough for skating. Received from home four photographs, groups of the school boys. Three of them are taken with part of the gymnastic apparatus and the wall for a background. The fourth is Mr. Moore[14] at the harmonium (in the open air) with the choir boys around him. The broken chilblains are getting better, I think. There is a new skin formed over one of them, the other I have not looked at. This is Pancake Tuesday.

There is an old legend which the boys circulate to their young and credulous companions. It is—that the sanctuary knocker[15] on the north door of the Cathedral vomits pancakes as soon as it hears one o'clock strike on Shrove Tuesday. I have heard that little boys have been seen to take baskets to receive the pancakes. Perhaps somebody has been there today for that purpose, for when I went to service this afternoon, the knocker had traces of snowballs on it which may have been thrown by some youngster in revenge for his disappointment.

26 Ash Wednesday. Dr. Armes not at service to-day. Snow melted away.

28 Harmony lesson by myself at Dr. Armes' tonight. John had to go to a practice at the Castle.

March 1 They are learning some of the Passion Music [Bach]. Harmony lesson with John at Dr. Armes' tonight. Counterpoint before dinner and duets after.

2 Judges at service this morning. Played the in-voluntary, an introduction to one of Rinck's Fugues.[16] Long service, from 10.30 a.m. to 1.15 p.m.

3 Dull, damp weather. More chilblains.

5 Tried some of the music for tomorrow night at Dr. Armes'.

6 Musical Society's Meeting. Good many members there. They are learning good music—some of Handel's Choruses, Mendelssohn's part songs, etc.

7 John's birthday. Gave him a little prayer book. Went to his house for tea and attended the Castle practice as he has to go to Dr. Armes'.

8 Castle Concert. Mr. Copeman sang a song, and was encored. We played Zauberflöte, Mozart, and part of a nocturne, Spohr.

1873, March: Aged 14

9 Judges at service again this morning. Came in rather late. I had to play ten minutes.

10 John gone to Yorkshire for a week. Nice morning. Left at morning service to myself. Boyce in C and "Incline Thine Ear"—Himmel.[17]

11 Did morning service—Turle in D and "Look Down From Heaven"—Kent.[18]

12 Did morning service—Chant. Ben.ite and Jub* [i.e. Benedicite and Jubilate], and "I Will Arise"—Creyghton.[19]

13 Did morning service—Hopkins in B♭[20] and "Try Me O God"—Nares.[21] Went to Musical Society tonight. Transposed "Then Round About the Starry Throne"—Handel, into E♭ and E.

14 Morning service—Chant.

15 Morning service—Marsh in D[22] and "All People"—Tallis.

16 The Rev. Hitchcock preached at the Cathedral this afternoon. Went to Bow Church at night.

17 Fred's nineteenth birthday. Written to him. John back. He says he heard Bach's Passion done by Halle's band[23] at Manchester when he was away last week. Confirmation lesson this morning under Mr. Rogers.

18 Fair weather. Coal not so scarce now. Their prices have lowered. Duet with J.W. at Dr. Armes'. Played the Judas Maccabeus chorus as duets from the simple piano score.

20 Played a very difficult service this morning—Croft in A.[24] Did fairly, but experience is the great thing for services. I want more stability as regards time. Musical Society Meeting. Attendance good. Music—"Mourn ye Afflicted" and "O Father Whose Almighty Power" from Judas Maccabeus, "May no rash Intruder" from Solomon, "May-day"—Muller, "The Swallow", "The Lark" and "Hunter's Song"—Mendelssohn.

21 Duets with Dr. Armes.

1873, March: Aged 14

22 Practiced tonight's duets on my piano this afternoon. Trial for four vacant singing boys places. About fifty boys tried. Those who got in were—Garsfield, Taylor, Dobson of Whitburn, and Pattison. The Castle concert was held in the divinity room tonight. This is the last of this term. A great number of ladies present. Played Zampa[25] and Hummel's Nocturne in F. Archdeacon Bland was there. He told me he was going to Alnwick soon and would try and see Father.

23 Martin came into the organ loft. Sermon by the Bishop of Dover this afternoon. The four new boys have commenced today.

24 Confirmation lesson this morning. With John at Dr. Armes' tonight. The Schubert duet, Market chorus [Masaniello] and some of the Judas Maccabeus choruses.

26 Our first counterpoint lesson with Dr. Armes, at noon today. Had a walk with John up the Observatory Hill. Enjoyed it very much. The sun shone brightly. The Cathedral looked beautiful from the place where we sat down.

27 Musical Society. Music—First three Judas Maccabeus choruses, Market chorus from Massaniello, "Then Round About the Starry Throne" and "Galatea Dry Thy Tears"—Handel.

28 The weather has been charming, the last three days. We can heartily enjoy the sun after so much dull, heavy weather.

29 Counterpoint at John's before dinner. Duets here after. Duets with John at Dr. Armes' tonight. Two of the Schubert's—March Heroic[26] and Grand Rondo.[27]

30 Weather very fine. Not well tonight. Have a headache, going to bed soon.

31 Last night's good sleep has put me all right. There has to be a voluntary after the Psalms in the evening as well as morning in future.

April 1 Fine day. Went to Dr. Armes' with John to do two more treble parts of "Hear My Prayer"—Stroud.[28]

2 Writing again this afternoon. Dyke's Communion Service in G.[29]

1873, April: Aged 14

3 Writing again. Grammar School Sports. Musical Society—First five Judas Maccabeus choruses, Drinking Song and Lark—Mendelssohn, Wreath—J. Benedict, and Market Chorus from Massaniello—Auber.[30]

4 Writing again. Several showers of rain during the day.

5 They have commenced putting the new organ[31] up. Writing again.

6 Long service this morning.

7 Fred's examination at Berwick.[32] It was to have been at Newcastle and I was going to meet him there, but he received an order to go to Berwick. I hope he will pass well. I had a bit of jumping with Martin at noon. It is capital exercise. Vic shot this morning at Offal. Poor dog.

8 Counterpoint lesson with John at Dr. Armes'. Second order of two part counterpoint for next time. Piano tuned by Mr. Hiller. The Litany, Responses, etc., done in monotone this week. Sermon this afternoon by Rev. Smith of the Training College.

9 Sermon by the Rev. T. Rogers. Paid Mr. Hiller 5s. He will tune four times a year in future for 15s.

10 Passion Music, half-an-hour's selection, this afternoon. It seems to have been received very well, although Bach is rather classical for the common run of people.[33] The Dean made a nice little address before it was begun.

11 Played this morning's service. Chants and "O Saviour of the World"—Goss. Sermon in the morning by Rev. Lowe, evening by Canon Eade. ***Good Friday.***

12 Met Father and Mr. Lawson on the Broken Wall about a quarter-past-eleven this morning. I did not expect him till the afternoon. Father looks very well.

13 "Worthy is the Lamb"—Handel, this afternoon. Sermon both morning and afternoon by the Dean. Father invited to Dr. Armes for dinner. I was invited also, but Father did not hear Dr. Armes say so. ***Easter Day.***

14 Got leave for today. Had a walk with Father and Mr. Lawson on to the Race Course. Men were playing at Pitch-and-Toss, and all sorts of things

1873, April: Aged 14

when we got there. Father has examined my Latin as far as I have done. He went away by the 4.40 p.m. quick train. Would arrive home at about 6.40 p.m.

15 Went for a walk with Whitehead nearly to Bear Park. The weather was warm like a summer day. Duets with John at Dr. Armes'.

16 They are beginning to tune the new organ now.

17 Rev. J. Lawson and family here today. Fine day. John is trying to put an organ part to an anthem composed by one of his Yorkshire friends. Musical Society.

18 Counterpoint lesson with John Whitehead under Dr. Armes at 3 o'clock this afternoon. Third Order for next time. Fine weather.

19 The Rehearsal was held in the nave with the new organ, this morning. The organ echoes terribly. You can hear the sound some time after taking the hands off. It is so many large pillars I suppose.

20 Very fine weather. Mr. Barnby officiated at St. Cuthbert's tonight. Mr. Ridley has gone from home for some time.

21 Weather still warm and fine. Tonight it has turned rather cold and dull.

22 Cold weather. Had a walk with Martin on the hill at 7 o'clock this morning. Sad occurrence next door. Mrs. Brown, when she came home at noon, found her husband hanging in the passage. The unfortunate man belongs to a family of unsound mind.[34] He was all right and cheerful at 9 a.m. Martin, Whitehead and myself at Dr. Armes' before and after dinner making out single parts of "God Save The Queen" for the Musical Society. Mr. Lawson's Birthday. The organ-builders have gone away I hear.

23 Little more copying at Dr. Armes' with Martin before dinner. Although the weather was showery this afternoon, and did not promise well [for the paper-chase], it was fine this afternoon. John and Walton started with five minutes start at 1.30 p.m. John's bag of papers was very big and clumsy. We went by the Observatory down to Stone Bridge along by the Brownie, etc. We had to scamper through it once. They were caught after four miles. Jimmie had got John to sit down with him through persisting that it was of no use, they would soon be caught,

Plate 1 Duke of Northumberland's School, Alnwick: pupils at physical exercise; Thomas Collinson senior in centre

Plate 2 T H Collinson's father in uniform of Northumberland Militia

Plate 3 T H Collinson's father

Plate 4 T H Collinson's mother, Hannah Sophia Gore

Plate 5 T H Collinson, aged 13 (standing)
with cousin Richard

Plate 6 T H Collinson, aged 17

Plate 7 T H Collinson as a young man

Plate 8 Dr Philip Armes, organist of Durham Cathedral

Plate 9 Dr J B Dykes, vicar, St Oswald's Church, Durham

Plate 10 Canon Greatorex, Precentor of Durham, 1862-1872

Plate 11 Canon Thomas Rogers, Precentor of Durham, 1872-1884

Plate 12 Durham Cathedral from the River

Plate 13 The Nave, Durham Cathedral, looking east

Plate 14 Bishop's Throne, Durham Cathedral; (right) South organ case

Plate 15 Durham Cathedral from Railway Station

Plate 16 Prebend's Bridge and Cathedral, Durham

Plate 17 The Sanctuary Knocker, Durham Cathedral

Plate 18 Interior, St Mary's Cathedral, Edinburgh

1873, April: Aged 14

John having such a clumsy bag. Well, when Kennedy and some of the others came nearly up to them, Jimmie sprang through a hole in the hedge, beside which he had been careful enough to sit, and left John with both bags vainly trying to get through a gate which would not open. After they were caught, and all got together, Brown and Kennedy set off. We soon lost the tracks as they had got into the old one. Hopper and somebody else who had stayed behind a bit did manage to follow them, but we lost scent completely. When we were consulting on the road a little beyond Stone Bridge, Jimmie Walton suddenly hushed us and made us cower down to let the two boys come nearer without seeing us. When we were all squatting down he said, "What a lot of fools!"

Aged 15

24 My birthday (15). Received nice letters from Father, Mother, Fred and a neat letter-case made of leather from Sam with a note inside. John gave me two books of Best's compositions for the organ.[35] I am very pleased that everybody has remembered me so kindly. I have great reason to be thankful that all amongst whom I am placed are always so kind to me. I wish I were more deserving. Shifted into the nave this morning. The new organ is very sweet, has a good deal of power. Some of the reeds were out of tune tonight. Musical Society. Practiced the principal things for the concert next week.

25 Cold, snowy weather. Dr. Armes gave Whitehead, Martin and me two tickets each for the Concert.

26 Counterpoint lesson with John under Dr. Armes this afternoon. The doctor tuned the new organ reeds[36] at 8 p.m. John blew and I put the keys down. My piano key fits the latch of the organ.

27 Received my usual weekly letter from Mother, although she wrote on my birthday. There was a nice little letter from Charlie Mattison enclosed.

28 Windy weather. Got up at 6 a.m., had a walk, or rather a run. I ran from the second stile on the hill round by the other side of the railway.

29 Weather fine, but very windy. I should think it will be healthy. Had a run again this morning. Same way. Running warms me up nicely. I am looking forward to another paper-chase.

1873, April: Aged 15

30 Got up at 5.30 a.m. Wrote a letter to Sam, had a run and went to the Cathedral at 7.30 a.m. Mr. Rogers and the Doctor took out all the choir organ pipes of the old organ.[37] I had to hold down the notes. Got away for breakfast at 9.30 a.m. Whitehead took the morning practice. Weather warm and balmy. The trees are budding. The Doctor took unwell this evening. I wrote to Fred and Mother in the afternoon. I just got the letter posted in time. The carrier came up to the branch box at the top of the North Road exactly the same time as I did. The time is very convenient. If I post a letter in a branch box by 3 p.m. they will receive it at home by about 8.

May 1 Musical Society Concert (Private).[38] Large, fashionable audience. Everything went off well. John and I played a piano duet—Grande Marche Heroique, Schubert. The Dean made a little speech at the conclusion. The piano was Mr. Hiller's. A German Trichord.

2 John brought his friend, Giles, who came yesterday, into the organ-loft this morning. Fine weather.

3 Dr. Armes tuned the reeds at 5 o'clock this afternoon. Whitehead and two boys went in with him. I went on with the practice and music boys.

4 Nice day.

5 Got up at 4.45 a.m. Had a walk in the rain to the plantation this side Bear Park. Got a few primroses.

6 Wet weather. Rather finer towards evening. Counterpoint lesson by myself with the Doctor tonight. Fifth Order for next time.

7 Went to the Cathedral at 7.15 a.m. The Doctor was there. I assisted in putting the pipes in different lots on the ground as they were handed down. We cleared the swell.[39] It had a great number of pipes. I did not get my breakfast till after service as Whitehead did not come to practice. Fine day. I think Mr. Rogers has gone from home. Enclosed a short note to Fred to congratulate him on having passed his Berwick exam.

8 Went early to the old organ.

1873, May: Aged 15

9 Fine day. Concert in the Town Hall tonight. Got up by Signor F. Martini and Mr. Lambert. John is accompanyist. Has a solo to play. I have not gone.

10 Went with John to have a look at his Father's allotment before dinner. Very fine day. "The Arm of the Lord"—Haydn, this afternoon. First time I have heard it done. Counterpoint lesson with John under the Doctor. The Doctor has got a new piano.

11 Fine weather.

12 T.W.B. called me up at 5 a.m. We went to Bear Park. Got a lot of cowslips and some primroses, violets, etc. Very fine morning. Enjoyed the walk very much.

13 Rose at 4 a.m. Went alone to Bear Park. Got some flowers. When I left the ruins to come home I felt sick, then dizzy and could hardly see the ground and was not able to walk steadily. I called at the farmhouse and asked for a little water, but the good woman very kindly took me in and made me some hot tea and bread and butter. Fine weather. Rather cold for the season. The trees are beginning to look nice and green again. T.W.B. and I tried to write an essay on "Essay Writing" tonight.

16 John away this afternoon. He has to go with some of the singing-men to a concert at Birtley[41] tonight. Wet weather.

17 Wet weather. Fred sent me a little letter yesterday enclosing some powder and pills. Counterpoint with John at the Doctor's this afternoon. Finished two part counterpoint. First order in three parts for next time. Went to St. Cuthbert's at night. John tried to tune the hautboy. He managed very well.

18 Wet all day.

19 Got up at 4 a.m. Weather getting fine again. Still cold though.

21 Fine day. Went to the Doctor's tonight. He told me to practice the oboe parts and vocal leads in the "Judas" choruses[42] on the harmonium out of the full score. I did not manage very well.

22 ***Ascension Day.*** The children of the principal church schools in Durham have a custom of coming to the Cathedral Morning Service on

1873, May: Aged 15

Ascension Day. Splendid anthem this afternoon—"Worthy is the Lamb"—Handel. I do not think I have seen the Doctor play so well before. I think the new organ is mellowing. The old organ is all away now. The pipes are in the library and the case, some in the treasury and some in the triforium, I think. Fine afternoon.

23 John Whitehead and I tried the Judas choruses at the Doctor's tonight on the piano and harmonium. I had to play the hautboy parts and bring all leads on the harmonium from the large score. Dr. Armes was drilling the riflemen[43] on the Palace green tonight.

24 Counterpoint with John under the Doctor this afternoon. Second order of three part counterpoint for next time. Had a walk with T.W.B. tonight by the Browney.

25 Warm weather. Had a stroll along Bear Park direction with John this afternoon.

26 Got up at 4.30 a.m. Partial eclipse of the sun. It began at 7.40 a.m., disappeared at 9.32 a.m. The moon seemed to come in front of the right hand of the sun near the top. It went gradually across to the left hand. Had a walk with T.W.B. along the Browney. Very nice weather.

27 John not well this afternoon. He would not ask the Doctor to let him go home though. Fine morning, cold in the afternoon. I can play "O Sing unto the Lord"—Greene,[44] from the score. The first movement is for five voices.

28 Fine day. Enclosed a note to Sam. Persuaded John to stopp [*sic*] off this afternoon. I took the practice and music boys. There is a cricket match on between the Durham and Hull men.

29 Royal Oak Day. Fine weather. The Doctor has a sore foot, and cannot pedal. John is rather better, but he did not come into the organ-loft so I have had all the work to myself today. Morning service—Goss in F, and "Sing Joyfully"—Byrd. Evening—Goss in E and "Our Soul is Escaped"—Walmisley (part of it). The choir sang three anthems on the tower.[45] "Lord, for thy tender"—Farrant[46](?), "Therefore with Angels"—Novello,[47] and "Give peace in our time"—Calcott.[48] I stood in the cloisters to listen. I heard very little of the second one as some children were scampering about. The singing began immediately after 5 p.m.

5. Kepier Hospital (in environs of Durham)

1873, May: Aged 15

30 Had tea with John. He took me along the old goods railway to Kepier Wood. Got some forget-me-nots, broom, etc. When I got home at about 9.20 p.m., I found Mr. Antony Graham had called to see me. I went down to the "Three Tuns" and had a chat with him. He expects to spend Sunday in Alnwick. He set me up home and Mr. Lawson went out with him back, part of the way. The boys and Whitehead, Martin and myself, had our portraits taken in group this afternoon by Mr. Heaviside. Fine weather.

31 Fine weather. John and I had a lesson on the piano and harmonium for the Musical Society concert next Thursday. I have to play the harmonium in some of the solo parts as well as in the choruses of Judas Maccabeus. We have a good many wild flowers in the house just now. The two young plantain (?) trees that I set in the back-yard the other day are progressing favourably.* Counterpoint lesson with John at the Doctor's tonight. Third order in the Three Part Counterpoint for next time.

June 1 Wet weather, especially at the fore-part of the day.

2 ***Whitsunday*** Got up at 5 a.m. Fine day. Sports in Wharton's Park. Went with John a walk to Sherburn Hospital this afternoon. Enjoyed it very much. No practice tonight.

3 Went to Dr. Armes' at 3 p.m. and had a practice with John at the "Judas".

5 Musical Society's Private Concert in the Town Hall. Everything went satisfactorily. Some of the solo parts in the First Part of Judas Maccabeus were omitted. This is the last meeting of the season. The boys, John, Martin and myself were to have had our portraits retaken this afternoon, but it was put off till tomorrow.

6 Went up to the Militia Barracks at 4 p.m. for Dr. Collins. Fine day.

7 Dr. Armes not at rehearsal and service this morning, his foot is worse. John brought his uncle into the organ-loft this morning.

* Janet Foster, author and journalist (see p xii), observes: These could be *Platanus hispanica*, the London Plane (a hybrid), Octopus Book on *Trees*. The only plantain *tree* is tropical.

1873, June: Aged 15

8 ***Trinity Sunday***. Fine day. Had a walk by the Browney with Martin and Smith this afternoon.

9 Rose at 6 a.m. Went to the Cathedral at 8.15 a.m. and played at cricket with the boys till 9 a.m. Fine weather.

10 Fine weather.

12 Mozart duet with John at the Doctor's.

13 Made two treble copies of "God is our Hope"—Aldrich.[49] Wet morning, fine afternoon and evening.

14 Fine day. Miners' Demonstration on the race-course. Between 70 and 100 thousand people in Durham they say. There were about 100 colliery bands. Those I heard played very well indeed. Some were in uniform.

15 Got leave from the Doctor to go home.

16 Fine day. Started at about 11 a.m. Arrived home a little after 1 p.m. Found all well.

19 The boys broken up for six weeks. Nice weather.

22 Played at church today [Alnwick]. Played "Wedding March"—Mendelssohn out at night for Mr. H. Vernon. Mr. & Mrs. James Cunningham here for tea. They are going to Bristol, a Curacy there. James looks very thin and delicate with study.

23 Was Confirmed at the Old Church [Alnwick] this afternoon. About 200 candidates present. The Bishop gave us such an excellent address. Father gave me the Violincello today.

24 W. Biggs and I walked to Alnmouth this afternoon. Had a bathe, tea at Wilson's, walked home again.

25 Went with Fred and T. Pickard and H. Brown to Alnmouth by train. Went on to the rocks, got nearly wet through with rain, had a bathe in the afternoon. Got home about 12 p.m.

27 Came back to Durham at night, about 11 p.m. when I arrived at Mr. Lawson's.

6. St Oswald's Church, Durham

1873, June: Aged 15

29 Sam's 21st Birthday. He was to start for Nottingham tonight. Mr. Moore goes as far as Derby with him on his way home. Played at St. Cuthbert's this morning.

30 I have a cold. I caught it at Alnmouth on Thursday, I think.

July 1 Got up late.

2 Took St. Cuthbert's practice tonight for John.

3 Three lady visitors, relations of the Lawsons', here today. Terrible gust of wind and rain about 5.15 p.m.

4 Mr. Lawson's visitors gone away tonight.

6 Took Sacrament for the first time at St. Cuthbert's. I liked the Communion Service very much.

7 Wrote to Sam this afternoon. Hope he will come on Wednesday.

8 Whitehead's cousin, Robert from Delph, arrived this afternoon.

9 The boys' treat to the Bishop's.[50] John and I went with them. The Brake started about 11 a.m.; arrived at the Palace at 1.05 p.m. There are some magnificent oil paintings in the Dining Room. There are the founders of the Israelitish Tribes. After dinner we had croquet, trap-bat-and-ball, and jumping, on the lawn. Strawberries at 4 p.m. Then I went to the hay field and raked for half-an-hour. We had tea at 6 p.m. when there was a bunch apiece of roses, etc. by the side of the plates, and the Bishop kindly gave each 2/6d. We left the Palace, much delighted with all that had occurred, at 6.45 p.m.; arrived home about 9 p.m.

10 Weather is exceedingly fine just now. It is nice for the hay.

11 Met Sam at the station at 6 a.m. The train was more than half-an-hour late. He was rather tired with travelling all night and so much holiday-making seems to have knocked him up. He went with me to morning service. We met John and Robert in Canon Jenkin's entry. After service, Mr. Lawson and the four of us went along the Triforium, where we saw the woodwork of the old organ, and up to the top of the South-Western Tower. Then back again, after we had been close to the Jesse

1873, July: Aged 15

window,[51] up the Lantern Tower to the Bells. We stood close to the Bells when 12 o'clock struck. The noise, especially of the big bell,[52] was awful. It is so large that you can stand under it. Robert once did when they were striking. Then we went on to the top,[53] and came down again, looked over the Library, and came home to dinner. I counted 324 steps in the Lantern Tower. Mr. Hiller tuned the piano in the afternoon. It did not take him long. It has stood well this time. Saw Sam off at 4.50 p.m. Very much disappointed he has made so short a stay.

12 Charlie Morrell called about one o'clock this afternoon. We had a walk round by Neville's Cross and up to Gilesgate Station where he had to call. Then we went to the Cathedral and ascended the Tower. He stayed service, had tea with me, and left for Fencehouses[54] where he is stopping, about 7 p.m.

13 I think all had gone right at St. Cuthbert's practice on Wednesday night. Robert played for them.

14 Written to Martin, and Mrs. Rushforth[55] to thank her for sending me a present of half-a-crown by Sam.

16 Enclosed a letter to Fred with Mother's letter. John and Robert at Newcastle. Played at St. Cuthbert's choir practice.

17 Saw Robert off at 11.20 a.m. Rain all the morning.

18 Militia returned from camp this afternoon. Dr. Armes has come back with them I hear.

19 Mr. W. Lawson's family from London arrived this afternoon. Mr. William has gone to Switzerland for a tour.

20 Played at St. Margaret's[56] tonight. The organ is very decent. Two manuals, one pedal stop, good great open,[57] two swell reeds,[58] etc., etc. In the Nunc. Dim. they chanted the canticle itself minor and gloria major. Dr. Armes is much sunburnt. He came to church this morning.

23 Had an hour's boating this afternoon with the Lawsons. Thunder storm this morning.

24 Spent the evening on and about the water with John and Garland (York deputy organist) and some of his friends. We had a nice chat with him

1873, July: Aged 15

about musical matters. He intends trying at Oxford for the Mus. Bac. preliminary soon. Dr. Armes is away at the choir festival at home [Alnwick] today. Mr. Rogers will precent and the Doctor conduct. I should have liked to have been at home. A niece of Mr. Lawson's here tonight to stay for two days. The house is pretty full.

25 Garland in the organ-loft this morning. He played in very nicely, extempore. He went away at 12. Weather cooler than it was a few days ago. I suppose the lightning the other day did much damage. Operated fatally in some cases.

26 Mozart duets with John at Dr. Armes'.

27 Took Sacrament at the Cathedral this morning. Played at St. Margaret's at night.

***August* 3** Played at St. Oswald's morning and evening.

4 Went to Newcastle at 8.30 a.m. Got there at about 9.15 a.m. Had to wait until 11 a.m. before the Alnwick trip came in. Mother did not come, but Father and Sam and Fred came, and St. Paul's choir. W. Biggs was there too. I saw several old friends, R. Nicholls, Tuck Hardy, etc. Went to the Museum. The collections of birds stuffed, shells, eggs, etc. are very fine. After dinner, went by boat to Tynemouth. Had a ramble about the battery priory, etc. with Father, Mr. Perry and Mr. Green, the new curate, and W. Biggs. Tea at 5 p.m. Returned by train to Newcastle. Saw them off at quarter-to-seven p.m., had a chat with R. Goodfellow and returned home at 7.25 p.m. The weather was for the most part wet, but it happened to be fine when we were outside.

6 John and I went with St. Cuthbert's choir in a brake to Castle-Eden.[59] Started at 8.30 a.m., arrived there at 10.30 a.m. The Black-Hall Rocks are very fine. They are full of magnificent caverns. We had a splendid dinner on the grass at 1 p.m. There was salmon, lamb, ham, etc., etc. I enjoyed it very much just after a bathe. John, one of the ladies, Miss Coldcleugh, and I had a sail. It was nice, I was leaning over the bow when a wave came and wet me through. Tea at 5 p.m. Started homewards about 8.30 p.m., arrived in Durham about 10.40 p.m. having thoroughly enjoyed the trip out. The weather was very nice, it looked rather cloudy once or twice, but that passed off.

1873, August: Aged 15

7 Nice weather. The Doctor has gone to London for a few days.

8 Wet evening. Have a cold. It is getting better now, but it was very troublesome a few days ago. Saw Macfarren[60] on the Doctor's piano tonight. I wish I had it back. Will ask again for it.

9 The Doctor was to arrive home again with the ten-minutes-to-five p.m. train today.

10 Weather fair, but cloudy looking. Sat reading this afternoon till a minute to four. Went to the Doctor's house at five to apologise. He was not in, but I saw Mrs. Armes. My watch stopped suddenly a week or two since at 9 a.m. It had been wound up all right the night before and when I tried it with the key it had three turns. I wound it up again, but it would not go. I think it must want cleaning. It has gone all right since I came to Durham. Mr. W. Lawson came here last midnight from his Switzerland tour. He had fine weather when he was there. Said the sun was very hot, but the air itself was not hot. In the houses they have venetian wooden blinds outside the windows which they keep almost closed making the room dark. One church he was in, the windows on the sun side were entirely shut in with common wooden shutters, the north windows being open. At one time Mr. Lawson walked a good many miles through the clouds, could see very little. Another time he was playing snowballs with the others and the sun was very hot. Some had umbrellas up when walking along the melting snow, the sun had such power.

11 Dr. Armes, after morning service, gave John, Martin and I[61] some music. I got Beethoven's Sonatas, miscellaneous pieces, and variations, three books of Haydn, Clementi's Gradus[62] and several operas. He also gave me Macfarren back without my asking.

12 After morning service the boys and the three apprentices went in a brake to Black-Hall Rocks, Castle Eden. Mr. Rogers did it at his own expense. We got there about 1 p.m. While dinner was being prepared I went with Gryce to explore every cavern or hole we could find. We had a delightful ramble. Some of the caves were very fine indeed. The tide happened to be out then so we could get right round the corner. We went past what the Coast-guard pointed out on Wednesday as the smugglers' underground passage. The dinner was very nice. Little pies, sandwiches, apple-puffs, lemon-cheese-cakes, etc., etc. There was lemonade, beer, etc. Gooseberries for dessert. After dinner we played

1873, August: Aged 15

at cricket on the sand with our boots and shoes off, a hint which Mr. Andrews, a friend of Mr. Rogers', gave us. Then we had a bathe and Mr. Rogers made races, etc. for nice prizes. One new race was this—He made two moderate sized rings on the sand and set out two lines of six or seven stones opposite each other from these rings. Each stone was a few feet off its neighbour. The two competitors standing ready at the rings, at the signal, rush at the stones one by one, depositing them inside the ring. He who put fewest stones inside the ring or took the most time in the operation, lost. Mrs. Rogers and the other ladies gathered sticks, boiled the kettle and made a nice tea for us all. After a few more games we started home at 7 p.m. as it was raining. It rained all the way, but nearly all had overcoats. I had my waterproof. We arrived home safely about half-past-nine having enjoyed ourselves very much, thanks to the kindness of the Precentor.

13 Fine weather. It is gradually losing warmth, though, I think. Counterpoint lesson with the Doctor. John could not go as he had St. Cuthbert's practice to go to. Three-part syncopation for next time.

17 Took Sacrament at the Cathedral.

19 The old organ pedals are on the Song-school organ now. Durham Flower Show on the Race-course. There has not been one for about 12 years here they say. It is a new committee. I did not go. Thomas Atkinson, the organ blower, got about 20 prizes for garden stuff, etc. Piano lesson tonight. Beethoven's miscellaneous pieces, bagatelles and the Rondo in C. Mr. Lawson has made up two melodies of hymn-tunes. He hummed them over and I put them down on paper and harmonised them. I like one of them very much. The other is too ranty for my taste. They are both triple time L.M.[63] in the key of F. Taken my watch to Burnett, the watchmaker, to be cleaned.

20 Took St. Margaret's choir practice for Mr. Richardson.

21 Nice day. Got my watch. It cost 2/6d. for cleaning.

22 Durham Agricultural Show. Wrote home to congratulate Father on his birthday, which was on the 19th. I am sorry I forgot till now.

23 John and I finished three-part counterpoint today. Will start with four parts for next time. I think it is a good plan going on by ourselves ahead of the Doctor; it grounds us well before we do it with him.

1873, August: Aged 15

24 Weather very agreeable. Not too hot.

25 Wet weather. There is a review at Lumley Castle today. Dr. Armes has gone, I think. Went up to the Round Window.[64] The new stained glass is very fine indeed. In the Centre is our Lord, round him in a circle are the twelve apostles, and round them are the twenty-four elders with harps in their hands. Good anthem tonight—"The Horse and his Rider"—Handel.

26 Very fine, warm day. There was a thunderstorm during the night. I was awake; the lightning was bright and frequent.

27 Played at St. Cuthbert's practice.

28 Played over Monday and Tuesday's anthems to the Doctor on the piano tonight. He will be away I suppose.

29 John went to Delph this morning for a fortnight. I hope he will enjoy himself. Poor fellow he has been bothered with toothache the last few days; will be a bad job if it sticks to him. Doctor left me to myself this morning.

31 Played at St. Cuthbert's.

September 1 Rifle competition at Kepier today. I believe Dr. Armes is there. I have the organ to myself today.

6 Went after morning service to the Doctor's to help to lay some sods in his lawn.

27 Went home this morning.

28 Played for Moore. He went to Ellingham church to play the new organ that was opened by Dr. Armes last week.

29 Michaelmas Day. General holiday in Alnwick. Mr. Edwin[65] drove us all out to Hulne Abbey[66] for the afternoon. We went nutting, but were very unsuccessful. Saw two or three squirrels. Fine weather.

30 Wet weather.

1873, October: Aged 15

October 1 Wet weather. Went to the meeting of the St. Paul's and St. Margaret's choirs [Alnwick] at the old church tonight. They had a very pretty little service altogether. They did Wesley's recit. in F and "Send out thy Light"—Gounod.[67]

2 Had Lewis in tonight and Tom Archibald and Harry Starwart. Lewis played Beethoven's big sonata in C[68], he plays from memory very well, and extemporizes very grandly.

4 Returned to Durham. Spent the afternoon in Newcastle. Met Matthew Dodd [old schoolmate] in the street. Just had a word or two with him. He is at Jarrow now having something to do with Lead mines or something of the sort. I went into the Town Hall. There was no organ recital as they were busy preparing for the concerts. Got home, after a wearisome day of it, about 6 p.m.

5 Had a walk in the afternoon with John.

13 Mr. Hiller tuned the piano. It has stood very well lately.

16 Went to Newcastle by the 5.10 p.m. train via Seamside to hear the "Creation".[69] Railway fare 2/3d. (3rd return). Gallery admission 1/6d. Soloists, Miss Rose Hersu, Mr. Whitehead and Mr. Aynsley Cook. Hersu and Cook did not arrive till the second and third parts respectively. They were preceded by Miss Penman and Mr. Ferry. I was very much pleased with the Oratorio. It is the first I have heard.

18 Counterpoint lesson with John at the Doctor's. Sam out of his time [i.e. out of his apprenticeship].

19 Walk with John. Mr. Lawson commenced term in the University for arts.

20 Accompanied at a concert given by five of our singing men at Chester-le-Street[70] tonight. Went in a cab. Supper after concert. Got home at 2 a.m.

21 Had supper with Anthony Graham. He is going home tomorrow, I think. He intends spending Sunday home at any rate.

22 Weather cold and wet, now and then.

1874, March: Aged 15

March 18 Long interval not entered. I will try and put a summary of the principal things I remember, being the most summary way of getting out of a difficulty.

I spent a very happy Christmas at home. We had a nice party in the school, in honour of Sam. Came back to Durham a day or two after New Year's Day. Sam went to Bruntnall's, Middlesbro', a short time after. Father spent a few hours with him and then came on to me. Went with John about six weeks since to hear Dr. Bulow[1] at Newcastle. It *was* a treat. It gave one such an insight into piano-playing. His memory was marvellous. To play all those sonatas, etc. was very wonderful. The price of admission was 7/6d. That we found out when we got to Newcastle. I sent Fred a little song of mine a week or two ago. He is pleased, I am rewarded.

Today we have had a fine paper-chase. John and Kennedy set off with nine minutes start. We went Offal way, then towards Stone-Bridge passing the "Kennels", across the field near Nevil's Cross, down the steep and muddy bank, over the Brownie, over again at the "Steppys", up "Clarty Lunnan", past "Arbor House" towards Bear Park, down to Aldon Grange Bridge,[2] where we were deceived by wrong scent, up homewards meeting the "hares" at "Three Tuns". The weather has been splendid. Even too hot at times. Poor Martin could not run. Sore leg.

19 University Sports. Wet and cloudy in the morning, but it got out fine in the afternoon. Felt a little stiff this morning from yesterday.

20 Wrote to Sam this afternoon. I have owed a letter for some time. The Doctor looked over our imitation tonight. We have to try double-counterpoint for next time, skipping the scholastic and curious imitations, as they are not exactly the most profitable for us just now.

21 Rather dull weather. Father has sent me, by tonight's post, the Musical Standards[3] for the beginning of this year.

22 Nice day. The Rev. Mr. Goe of Sunderland preached this afternoon.

23 Beautiful weather. Only a fortnight to Easter. University finished term today, I believe.

25 Service at 9 a.m. this morning. Alto trial. Four competed. Entwhistle, Lichfield; Stilliard, St. Paul's; Leatham, York; and Bates, Chester

1874, March: Aged 15

(formerly choir-boy here). Entwhistle was chosen. Bates was very little behind him. If his voice were a little fuller he would have got in as he is a good musician. Organ this afternoon, saint day.

26 Fine weather. Grammar School Sports. I saw two steeplechases and some flat races.

27 Wet and dull. Good go at Ouseley's harmony[4] tonight. It is a fine book.

28 Beautiful morning, wet afternoon. Trial for new boys at 11 a.m. Five appointed. Two of them to come next month.

30 Got up early. Nice morning.

31 John did not come to service or M.S. [Musical Society] tonight. Not well he says.

April 1 All Fools' Day. Posted a letter to W. Biggs.

2 Selection from Spohr's Calvary this afternoon. Went very well. Mr. Nutten, the basso came. Wrote to Charlie Mattison. Received a letter from Mother and Fred, and a beautiful Easter card. Fred is coming on Monday for two days. How nice.

3 ***Good Friday.*** Nice day. Mr. Lawson and nephew at Finchale in the afternoon.

4 Counterpoint at the Doctor's tonight. Double-counterpoint in the tenth[5] for next time.

5 ***Easter Sunday.*** Went to St. Oswald's early Sacrament with Mr. Lawson. Nice weather. New hymn of the Doctor's this afternoon.

6 Fred arrived about 11 a.m. Soon after we had got into the house, Sam and Harry Starwart came, to our surprise. We went to the Cathedral before dinner; and to Pelaw Wood to see the races, after. After service we went into the Library. Harry and Sam went off to Alnwick and Middlesbro' about 7 p.m. The weather was glorious till night, and then it rained hard. The station was crammed. We could not wait to see them off; could hardly get back again either.

7. Finchale Priory, near Durham

1874, April: Aged 15

7 Was late to practice this morning. The Doctor spoke about it for the first time. I was sorry it happened. Did not know the time was getting on so fast. Doctor has gone to London this morning. Fred, John, Malcolm and I went up the Tower at 11. Stood by the bells at 12 o'clock. Martin, Fred and I went to Finchale in the afternoon by Kepier Wood. Cloudy weather. Rain came on in the evening. John came to us at 6 p.m. We came home together soon after in the rain. We enjoyed the walk back though. Went on to John's house where he let us see some songs that would do for Fred. We are tired with the walking.

8 Fred went home at 9 a.m. this morning. I am sorry to part with him. He has left me a nice little book from Father—Mason's Self Knowledge. Nice day.

11 Miss Dalby and Mr. Jennings here for tea. John brought me across to the Organ Factory.[6] Mr. Harrison has a rather nice little organ ready for Sherbourne.[7] Two manuals; about eighteen stops.

12 Dr. Armes back again. Had an hour in the Factory this afternoon. John played some Mendelssohn's sonatas, etc. The stops are of a nice quality.

13 Piano duets with John at the Doctor's tonight. The most exquisite music I ever heard almost. Schubert Nocturne,[8] I believe it was.

14 Received a nice long letter from William Biggs. They are trying to get a full peal of bells at home. John is to sing at the Handel Festival. That's why the Doctor asked us last night what voices we had. It is in June, I think.

15 Very bad cold. Think I caught it in returning from Finchale in the rain, at night time too.

16 Written to Sam. This cold makes me feel all out of sorts. Bad head, etc.

17 Fine day. The Doctor doesn't seem well today. The piano is very nice, having been tuned yesterday. 15s. is due now to Mr. Hiller for one year's (4) tunings. A third batch of artillery in the town today.

18 Paid Mr. Hiller.

19 Played for Richardson at his church tonight. He wanted to go out and hear Mr. Harrison's new organ at Sherbourne. Fine day.

1874, April: Aged 15

20 Fine day. John not very well this morning. Mrs. Lawson unwell too. The weather must be doing it. Received a nice little letter from Charlie Mattison. He is at the Bank now, and likes it. Martin away yesterday and today.

21 As my cough is troublesome, the Doctor told me not to come to Musical Society tonight.

22 Very fine day. Quite warm. Called at the Post Office to withdraw 10/- from the bank. Mr. Lawson's birthday.

23 Beautiful day. How charming the Banks look. The opening leaves give such a varied effect. Those orchards in South Street banks look so nice with the white blossom. Scott at home for a fortnight. He looks well, and seems to like the school at Nottingham.

Aged 16

24 My birthday. Received three kind letters from Father, Mother and Fred, which I have answered. Fine day. Not so sunny.

25 Warm, but dull. Tried over, with John, the Hummel duet at Doctor's. We are to play it at the Musical Society Concert in May. We have a copy each.

26 Fine day.

27 Fine day. Very misty at night. Another lesson at the Hummel duet.

28 My cough very bad at service this afternoon. It was so miserable, because I didn't like to cough lest the Doctor should think I was only "making" to get away from Musical Society. Strangely enough, last Tuesday night I was unusually bad and the Doctor told me to stop indoors that night. He did the same tonight. Fred kindly sent me a letter with some lozenges—Ipecacuana.

29 Most beautiful weather. So warm and sunny. The fruit blossom in the South Street orchards has been very abundant this time. Sent Father, in today's letter, notes from the Leipzig Musical Conservatory Prospectus which Vincent[10] lent me the other day. It must be a fine place for studying music. I feel much better today.

May 1 I have caught fresh cold. There is such a draught always at the North and South doors when they are opened for service; and once

1874, May: Aged 16

when I went to the Organ Loft, Thomas' door was wide open making an icy draught of air. John has gone to Castle Howard[11] to open an organ of Harrison's.

2 Nice walk with T.W.B. this afternoon. Fine weather. The scenery is beautiful.

6 Gone home. Father wrote to the Doctor for leave.

30 Come back again to Durham. I am much better now.

31 Fine day.

June 1 Nice day.

2 Wet this afternoon. I am very delighted with the study of botany. Balfour's book is very nice. Dick's microscope[12] is a very good one. I am glad Father let me bring it.

3 Nice day. Wrote home. I have begun German. I hope I will stick to it.

4 Wrote to Sam before dinner. Received one from him this evening. Fine day. Theory lesson for all three of us tonight. John, Berlioz;[13] myself, Counterpoint; Martin, Harmony.

5 Rather dull weather today. Men of politics here are all getting very bad tempered and excited. Mr. Greenwell[14] cannot master his spleen. His rabid speech seems to be getting the contempt it deserves. Had a good chat with C. Vincent at 11. I have to play at St. Oswald's on Sunday morning. Went tonight to see what music is to be done.

6 Charming weather. The Doctor touched up the flute as well as the reeds[15] tonight. Sam gone home tonight. He said in his letter the other day he thought of going, but would send a postcard. If I had known I would have gone up to the station to see him. I am so disappointed when I think he has been so near. How I know he came tonight is, a porter called at the door with a parcel from Sam containing—a Banjo! Just fancy. I hope he will enjoy himself and have nice weather. I should so like to be there at his entering home tonight. I can just fancy what it will be, after six month's separation. A nice letter from Mother tonight. The Bells subscription fund [at Alnwick] is progressing nicely.

1874, June: Aged 16

7 Fine day. Played at St. Oswald's this morning. Went a walk in the afternoon with John and Martin.

8 Charming weather.

9 Weather still the same. This sort of climate makes up for the extremely cold May that we had. Counterpoint lesson tonight. Have to write circular canons for next time. Martin and I did a little mowing after the lesson.

11 Parliamentary Election for the city of Durham. Herschell and Monck elected. Major Duncan and Barrington two better men in my opinion. There has been bribing again I hear. Extremely cold and very dull weather.

12 Charles Vincent came into the organ-loft with us this afternoon. Willis[16] is coming tonight I hear, to take measurements for the new organ.

13 Nice letter from home tonight. Sam is coming through on Monday.

15 Cold weather for June. Sam came and surprised me this afternoon. He went to service with us. Went to Middlesbro' at 7.30 p.m. The Doctor is going away as well as John, so I will have to play on Sunday.

17 John went to London tonight.

18 Doctor gone this morning.

20 Queen's Accession Day. Declaration of yesterday's poll. Palmer, Elliot and Bell. Sir George was only two behind Palmer. I am so glad.

4256
4254
4104

21 Three services on hand today. Rather heavy responsibility.

22 First day of the Regatta. A short, heavy shower at 3 p.m. Fine after. "Fixed" this afternoon's service. Went very well.

23 Fine weather. More interesting boat races, this afternoon. The band played very nice music. One piece, a sort of Fantasia, was very

1874, June: Aged 16

expressive and tasteful. Fire-works at night. They were very brilliant. Then rain in the evening, threatened to stop the affair, but it was fair later on.

27 The Doctor and John came back at 5 p.m. this afternoon.

28 The Doctor at church. I played Bach's "St. Ann's"[17] out, this afternoon.

29 John has lent me Macfarren's "Six Lectures"[18] to look at.

30 Boys' trip to Tynemouth. Mr. Lawson took charge of them. John, Martin and I went. Set off at 8.30 a.m. Went by boat from Newcastle at 10.30 a.m. Reached Tynemouth at noon. I got Martin, Pearson and Donaldson to have a row with me for an hour. The water was very smooth. Then I had a bathe. There was a good tea for all at 4.30 p.m. Part of us reached home at 8.15 p.m., others, having stopped in Newcastle, at 10.15 p.m.

July 1 I am sorry to find I have got a heavy cold again. The worst is, I am solely to blame for my carelessness. I hope it will not be very bad. I daren't tell Father and Mother. On Monday I heated myself a little, and yesterday the rain and splashing when in the boat, and sitting on the sand increased it a good deal.

2 Very fine, hot day. I am glad of the warm weather.

3 Dr. away for two days. Fine weather.

5 Still fine weather.

6 Short letter from Sam.

7 Rather dull weather this morning. Judges here this afternoon.

8 Fine, warm weather. Martin brought his violin and we had a bit of fiddling together.

9 Hot today. Mr. W. Reay, I noticed, was at service this afternoon. Martin brought his violin again tonight.

12 Had a short walk with Martin this afternoon.

8. Ordnance Survey Map of Durham (c.1870)

1874, July: Aged 16

13 Martin gone for three weeks holiday.

14 Saw the Comet[19] tonight. It is very bright.

15 How fine the weather still keeps. I think it is unusually dry and warm this summer. Orwin in the organ-loft this morning. He extemporizes very well indeed. I have the keys of the Market Church organ[20] as I have to play for Mr. Stimpson[21] on Sunday. We went into the church today and let Orwin try the organ. Harrison's have shifted it to the west end, it looks very imposing and sounds well. How much better than in that corner.

19 Played at St. Nicholas'.

26 Mr. Stimpson kindly made me a present of Dr. Marx[22] "General Musical Instruction".

27 Got up at 4.35 a.m. Letter from Sam.

28 Part of the choir gone to assist at the reopening of Ripon Cathedral.[23] Dr. Armes is to play I believe.

August 2 Nice day.

3 Nice weather, rather colder. Martin come back.

4 Wrote to Sam. School recommenced today at home. Wet day.

5 Wet again. This weather will be good for the gardens I should think. Wrote a few lines to Fred with Mother's letter.

6 A very fine day. Bright and windy.

7 Fine day again. Cloudy looking sometimes. Mr. Hiller tuned the piano this afternoon. It wanted it rather.

9 Sam has resolved to go to America. Sorry to hear it. Wrote him a long letter today against it.

11 Mr. Rogers' trip to Roker.[24] We three went as well. The brake started about 9 a.m. Took rather more than two hours to go. Had an excellent

1874, August: Aged 16

dinner; cricket, bathing, etc. in the afternoon. I did not bathe, the weather was so cold and rainy just then. It cleared up though towards tea time and afforded a most beautiful sight of the beautifully coloured clouds over the sea reflected by the setting sun. We started homewards soon after tea and arrived safe at about 9.30 p.m. Letter for me tonight from Mother saying Sam intends going with a fellow who has had four years at tree-cutting in America.

15 Sam, I am happy to hear, is not going after all. He was going to give Brentnall's a fortnight's notice tonight, but providentially, Mr. Robert Davidson of Alnwick met him in Middlesbro' and persuaded him to stay at home.

16 John Whitehead's cousin, Harry, who has been staying here a week, is going home tomorrow. He is an amiable lad. Splendid weather.

17 Lovely day.

18 The Doctor is going to name John for the appointment at Cornhill.[25] I wonder when he'll go—What shall I do without him? Nothing but to work hard and try to be as faithful an apprentice as he has been.

19 Father's birthday. Very hot weather. I forgot to post the letter to Father last night so it will not arrive till tonight. Our boys (choristers) are to have a cricket match today with Mr. Hall's school. Orwin called in this afternoon. We had a duet or two, etc. and an enjoyable walk. It was rather hot though.

20 Nice day. Cloudy looking though. The boys won easily by an innings and twenty-eight runs. The Doctor gave me a lesson in score playing tonight. He was very kind and encouraging. He gave me the scores of all Beethoven's String Quartetts, Trios and Quintetts.[26] It is an extremely handsome and useful gift. They are so nice to study and examine as well as play. What a rich depth there is in Beethoven's music! His piano sonatas are certainly splendid.

21 Nice day. Went to Mr. Harrison's this evening. Gave the little boy his first music lesson.[27] He is only going on for seven years of age, but I hope to make something of him as he is a very bright little fellow. I am pleased Mr. Harrison has asked me to bring him on, as it is a sort of interesting experiment in teaching. I will do my best to teach him

1874, August: Aged 16

carefully and make him a *musician* in the proper sense of the word, not to play like a machine or weaken his faculties on dance music, but to have some expression and some real knowledge of harmony.

22 Certainly the weather is glorious. Nice and hot for the harvest. Took a walk out this afternoon along Browney by Bear Park.

23 John, Martin and I had a short walk this afternoon.

25 Fine day. Flower Show on the Race Course. There were two bands, the Queen's Bays and a Yorkshire Band. I liked the first very much. The Yorkshire fellows of course were not so good, they were a good deal out of tune too. The show was very good as far as it went. This is only the second Flower Show they have had.

26 St. Cuthbert's choir trip to Marsden Rock today. We three apprentices went. Started by rail for South Shields at about 9 a.m. Had a good walk from South Shields station to the Rock, about three miles. There was a brake for those who preferred it. The cliffs are magnificent. The house is composed partly of rooms and partly of caves, one in which we had dinner. We got home about 11 p.m. Everybody seemed very happy. There couldn't be a more enjoyable treat. The weather looked terribly threatening till about 2 p.m. This had a grand effect over the sea. The sight was magnificent of the sea dashing and foaming wildly over the rocks, the cliffs overhanging so massively.

30 The Doctor is unwell. He complained of his side this morning. He stayed away this afternoon.

31 Nice weather again after last night's rain. Mr. Harrison has got the water-engine[28] today. Such a tidy [tiny?] little thing. Far smaller than I expected.

September 1 Wet morning, but it cleared up and got fine afterwards. Piano and Harmonium duets. I forgot to go till a quarter to nine.

2 Mr. Harrison's organ is nearly ready.

3 John brought some music with him to the Factory tonight, we had a nice bit of organ-playing. Two or three gentlemen and ladies were in to hear it. Some of the stops are delicious. That Vox Celestis and Echo Salicional[29] are quite fascinating.

1874, September: Aged 16

4 John has heard from the Cornhill Rector. Matters will soon be settled.

5 Got a letter from Sam this morning asking me to go and see him tonight and stay till Monday morning. Got leave from the Doctor. Went at 6 p.m. Got there about 7.45 p.m. He was at the Station. Waited a short time while he finished at the shop. Then we went for a walk with Miss Langley and Miss Lincoln.

6 Went with Sam to early communion, St. John's, 7 a.m. Morning service at 10.30 a.m. In the afternoon Miss Langley went with us into the Park, which is very beautiful. There was a good band of wood and brass. We had tea at the Langleys'. They are kind people, also very musical. Went to St. John's at 6.30 p.m. Splendid service. Singing and organ good (can't say that for the morning) very eloquent sermon. Quite ritualistic I could see. The preacher, Mr. Blair (curate) brought forth historical arguments in favour of ritualism which were very interesting. I was quite taken with the evening service. Nice walk after church. Miss Langley and Miss Chambers were with us.[30]

7 Left Middlesbro' at 9.25. I could have liked a day or two more. Wrote to W. Biggs. Doctor away somewhere with the Rifles.

10 I have to play at Ellingham on the 22nd at their Harvest Festival. Doctor has kindly made it into a fortnight's holiday, at which I am very pleased.

11 Received a letter from home with P.O.O. for £1. Paid Strathman's for the boots 12/-.

12 Went with John to St. Cuthbert's tonight. He let me try my hand on at tuning the hautboy.

13 The Rector of Bury[31] here today to hear John's playing. John played all but the anthem this afternoon. He is to go.

14 Nice morning. Gone home.

26 Come back again to Durham. Father came with me, saw the Doctor, and went on to Sam at night. I have had a most happy stay at home. The weather has been very fair. Ellingham Festival on 22nd went off well. Mr. Moore and I got there on Monday afternoon, had a practice with the choir at night. Next morning the Alnwick lot came in a brake. The organ is a splendid instrument of it's size. Gray and Davison.[32] Canon

1874, September: Aged 16

Evans preached in the morning, very eloquently. Mr. Moore and I had dinner with the singers at the school. A Mr. Maule (brother to Mrs. Cresswell) preached at night. Supper at the vicarage, then the brake took us home about midnight.

27 Nice afternoon. Father will have been at St. John's today with Sam.

28 Some chant-writing to do. The Doctor has revised the collection and put a lot of new ones in. Went to meet Father at 3 p.m. Sam came with him, to my surprise and pleasure. Father went home at 5.08 p.m. and Sam went back to Middlesbro' at 7.33 p.m.

29 Weather inclined to be wet today. Mr. & Mrs. Harrison are to come home tomorrow night. I gave Arthur a lesson tonight.

30 Alto trial this morning. Leatham of York Minster was appointed. Four tried. They were all bad readers, rather strange. Very fine day. It seems frosty tonight.

October 1 Wet day.

2 Weather wet at intervals. Mr. & Mrs. Harrison came home last night at midnight. Gave Arthur another lesson.

5 Rae's Concerts began again tonight. We three lads went. Doctor gave us leave from practice without being asked. I think perhaps he saw something was up as I had my top-coat on in service. The trains run nicely for us. There is a fast train at 5.08 p.m. and a slow by Leamside (takes an hour) at 5.25 p.m. Today we went by the 4.30 p.m. train which was very late here. The concert was very fine. I was charmed with Semiramide.[33] They did a Mozart symphony in E^{b} instead of Beethoven's first symphony in F.[34] The latter was announced in the morning's paper. It was cold waiting for the 11.23 p.m. mail.

9 Arthur did very well at his lesson tonight.

10 John has gone with Mr. Harrison to Hartlepool for the day. Wet weather. Tuned St. Cuthbert's reed tonight. Martin and "Fuss" went up with me. Received a box from home by railway, with two bottles of cod-liver-oil in.

1874, October: Aged 16

11 Went to Mr. Harrison's for dinner and he made me "finish up" by stopping all day with them. How very kind they are to me. The children are so nice and well behaved.

12 Dull looking today.

13 Mr. Hullah[35] came to the Musical Society tonight. He is an aristocratic-looking man. Mr. Foster made me have supper with him, as we came home together. He played two games of chess and beat me of course.

14 John has gone to play for Martini [Martini is correct; Martin is not intended here.] at Stockton tonight. I went to St. Cuthbert's choir practice.

16 Gave Artie Harrison his lesson. John and I had to go to Doctor's at 8 for piano duets.

17 I touched up the reed at St. Cuthbert's tonight. Pattison and Foster went with me.

18 Nice day. Had a short walk with Martin this afternoon.

19 We three went to Newcastle tonight. It was a splendid concert. Mendelssohn's Scotch Symphony was really wonderful. It put everything else in the shade. They did an overture of Rossini's—Gadha Lazzra,[36] or some such name, March from Tannhauser (Wagner) which I liked very much indeed; Fra Diavolo overture; selections from Lucia di Lammermoor; Strauss's Blue Danube waltz; etc. The weather has been very fine. Mr. Lawson has passed the first year exam, which was very stiff.

20 Rather dull looking and cold today.

21 Martin and I went to hear the Elijah tonight. We went by the half-past four express which came in here nearly half-an-hour late. The Doctor and Mrs. Armes went, also several Durham people. There was rather a crush at the gallery door. We first saw the "Roll Call" a most splendid picture [i.e. a painting], then went to the doors three-quarters of an hour before time, there being some people even then. The doors were opened somewhere about 7 p.m. and we got a nice seat for 1/6d. The oratorio was done very well on the whole. I thought the voices were

1874, October: Aged 16

inferior to the band. Vernon Rigby has a pleasing voice, but it doesn't sound so hearty and refreshing as Mr. Whitehead's; he did not pronounce his words over well.

23 Gave Artie Harrison his lesson tonight. John came up to Harrison's at 8 p.m. We had supper and duets.

24 Duet playing with Martin at the Doctor's tonight. With practice we will get on very fairly.

25 The new rule of sermons in the Sunday afternoons and service at 3.30 p.m. instead of 4 p.m. began this afternoon. The Archbishop of Canterbury preached a nice plain sermon. He has a good, deep voice.

27 Rather a hard practice at the Musical Society tonight.

28 There was organ this afternoon on account of today being the feast of Sts. Simon and Jude. I took the music boys tonight according to the Doctor's new order which he made last night. John has them on Tuesdays and Fridays, and I on Wednesdays and Saturdays. Weather dull and wet.

29 Wet, dull weather. My favourite service today—Hopkins in A.[37] It is so musical and expressive.

30 Gave Artie his lesson tonight.

31 Rather dull today. Duets with Martin at the Doctor's tonight. Martin is improving much in his playing.

November 1 Dull weather. Spent the day at Mr. Harrison's.

2 Heard from Sam this morning. He seems to be very well.

3 The Mechanic's Institute Jubilee begins today with an Exhibition at Alnwick. The Duke will preside tonight. I should like to be there.

4 There is a grand concert in the Town Hall, here, tonight. Miss Edith Wynne, Mr. and Madam Patey, Cummings, etc. I did not go.

1874, November: Aged 16

5 Guy Fawkes Day. There seem to be a few fireworks astir. John and I have commenced a system of fortnightly examinations between our two selves. We give each other questions with a set time to do them in.

6 Most beautiful, clear, refreshing day. We had to do some copying at a new Gibbons anthem—"O Lord, in Thy Wrath".[38] C. Vincent[39] seems to be getting on very well with his theory. His brother is at Leipzig. Gave Artie Harrison his lesson tonight. He got on very well indeed. I am quite pleased. Mr. Harrison is away at Castle Eden. Tonight John had a lesson in Berlioz and I a counterpoint lesson. There was not time to look over my exercises, so we have to go again tomorrow night.

7 John and I went to the Doctor's tonight. We played duets and the Doctor seemed to forget about my counterpoint, I am very sorry.

8 Had tea at Mr. Harrison's and went to St. Margaret's to play for Mr. Richardson.

9 Fair weather. Martin not well.

11 John gone with Mr. Rogers to Northallerton for a concert tomorrow. Frosty weather.

12 Found this morning that snow had fallen during the night.

13 John came back this afternoon. I gave Artie his lesson tonight. John and I went to have a lesson in the "Elijah"[40] work. John is to play the wind parts on the harmonium while I help the chorus a bit on the piano.

14 Glorious day. Almost like spring. T.W.B. and I went for a short walk before dinner [i.e. lunch], but we didn't land home till after 3 o'clock. We went by a roundabout way to the top of Brandon Mount, then round home by Brancepeth. Nearly twelve miles I should think. I took the music boys tonight and tuned St. Cuthbert's reed and had a little bit of practice. Heard from home as usual, tonight. The Exhibition has been a great success [cf. 3/11/74]. Father must have had some hard work over it. He made a nice little speech on Tuesday night at the closing, to return thanks for the vote of thanks to the committee.

15 Dull, sleepy day.

16 Mr. Hiller tuned the piano this afternoon. I heard from Sam tonight.

1874, November: Aged 16

18 I went to Mr. Richardson's choir practice tonight, [at St. Margaret's] then had supper with him.

19 Mr. Whitehead will see Father and Mother today as he has to go to Alnwick for a concert at Eglingham.

20 John and I went to work at the "Elijah" tonight. John manages the wind parts very well.

21 Fine, frosty day. Mr. Whitehead saw them [i.e. T.H.C.'s parents] at home. [He] spent some time there.

22 New honorary canon read in today. Mr. Hitchcock, vicar of Whitburn.

23 Cold weather. I have got over half a dozen chilblains just starting for themselves in a small way, on my hands. Heard from W. Biggs yesterday morning. His brother, John, has had a good voyage I am glad to hear.[41]

25 Mr. Harrison's Norham friend here, Mr. Green.

29 Another new honorary canon [appointed to Durham Cathedral], Mr. Martin, vicar of Newcastle.

December 2 Received a letter from S. Millar this morning. Very severe weather. Frost and snow.

3 Cold weather. I have got a slight cold. Wrote to S. Millar and sent him a kyrie and two chants.

1875

January 4 I have neglected my diary a long time. The Musical Society's Concert—"Elijah"— went off very well, on the 16th of last month. Dr. Armes gave John and I each a copy of Handel's Choruses (for the organ by Best). I was very pleased. I went home on the 18th and we were all unwell with colds, etc. W. Biggs finished his five years [apprenticeship] at Xmas. The Bells[1] were opened the day before Xmas. They are very beautiful. Sam came home on Xmas morning and brought Mr. Hermitage

1875, January: Aged 16

with him. We spent a very nice Xmas day all together. Poor Mother's cough was very bad though. On Boxing Day I returned to Durham. John left home on the 28th to stay a day or two at Delph and then go over to Bury. He had a nice presentation from the St. Cuthbert's people, in the shape of a gold watch and chain, ring and an inkstand. We miss him very much. On Saturday night (2nd Jan.) there were some terrible gas explosions near and *at* Martin's. At Gray's the tailor it was very sad, hurt more or less all the family, and one or two children are dead. Martin's did not get hurt, but a lot of furniture was damaged and Mr. Summers who, with his man near him, struck the match was sadly cut and his brain injured. Today (4th Jan.) Doctor went away for nearly a fortnight. It is dull without both John and the Doctor, and not seeing much of Martin. The river is swollen after the ice going. There has been a lot of skating. This winter has been a very severe one indeed, and the cold really intense.

5 Received a nice letter from John tonight. Poor fellow, he is unhappy of course, being entirely among strangers, but he will soon brighten up. I am glad he has such an excellent choir, ten men and twelve boys. He seems to have taken a fancy to his boys already. I went down the street and showed the letter to Martin and Mr. Whitehead. Mr. Whitehead had also just got a letter from John. Martin gave me Hamilton's Catechism on the Orchestra,[2] a very nice little present. We are getting on well together. Fred sent me about a gallon of Cod Liver Oil on Saturday night. I began it yesterday (Monday).

6 ***Epiphany.*** There was organ this afternoon. Difficult anthem—"Arise, Shine"—Greene.[3] Mr. Leatham tried his part in the song-school after morning service. I gave the boys a holiday from practice tonight. Martin and I went to St. Cuthbert's choir practice. Mr. Whitehead is still an indoor prisoner with his cough. I wrote a long letter to John this afternoon and enclosed him an aluminium pencil and pen. Damp weather tonight.

7 Dull weather. I let Reviley [probably a cathedral chorister] come into the organ-loft this morning. He seems a very musical boy. Four-part canons are difficult to do. I don't know what are the best intervals to imitate in. Brutton behaved very badly in practice tonight. I gave him and Sarsfield tasks, I don't expect Brutton will do his, but he must not get the upper hand. I have begun Berlioz by myself.

8 Dull weather. The boys got their prizes this afternoon in the Chapter-

1875, January: Aged 16

room. Mr. Rogers,[4] at 4 o'clock, spoke to me about my giving Brutton leave this afternoon and not having consulted him. He was quite right, but I gave the leave on the spur of the moment after much bother. Brutton will make the place too hot for him, [i.e. himself] as his behaviour in school and practice is very bad. Miss Dalby was here to tea, before returning to school tomorrow.

9 Dull weather. The Precentor gave Brutton a good talking to this morning, and told him to write his task twice out. Mr. Rogers came into the organ-loft tonight. He can extemporise very nicely, but his execution isn't clean enough for me. I went up to have some piano and violin duets with Mr. Whitehead tonight. Mrs. Whitehead has not returned yet, she has been poorly I am sorry to hear. I have begun sending John a bill [i.e. music list?] weekly. His present directions are 8, Bolton St., Bury, Lancs.

10 Dull weather. Martin played at St. Cuthbert's this morning. Nice anthem this afternoon—"Hear my Prayer"—Mendelssohn. Hyde sings the solo very nicely.

11 Dull weather. Stainer's "Lead, Kindly Light" this afternoon. I am very fond of it.

12 Poor old Mr. Moore[5] was buried at the Cathedral this morning. This severe winter has been too much for the old man. He seemed to retain a great love for Alnwick, and always when he met me, asked after "Canny Alnwick". Dull weather. The boys behaved very badly tonight. I saw the present proposed specification for John's organ today. I sent it by post to Mr. Harrison who is at Castle Howard this week.

13 Dull weather. Got up late. I think it is high time I tried to rise earlier. Wrote to John this afternoon and sent him a harmony and counterpoint paper to do. Sir Frederick Ouseley[6] was at service this afternoon. I just got a glimpse of him in the cloisters. The chants went very badly. I gave several boys tasks for misbehaviour tonight.

14 Fine day. The morning was rather dull, but the sun came out after and made it very cheering.

15 Wet day. I still got up very late. There was a gentleman at service this morning who, Martin felt sure, was Dr. Bridge.[7] I went to Mr.

1875, January: Aged 16

Harrison's tonight and began again with Artie after the holidays. Mr. Harrison came home from Castle Howard tonight when I was in.

16 Got up earlier. Mr. Lawson went to North Shields this morning. Sir Frederick Ouseley was at service again this afternoon. Doctor came home by the five train this afternoon. Done no theory today. I got on reading Wilson's Border Tales tonight and wasted a lot of time, sorry to say.

17 Very fine day; quite cheering. Old Mr. Ridley seems to be getting feeble in his voice. Sorry to say I did not attend his sermon this morning, and so most likely missed some very good advice. I am fond of his sermons; they are so homely and good. Had a short walk with Tom and William this afternoon and enjoyed it thoroughly. Last night the Precentor sent word to the effect that the service this afternoon would be at 4 o'clock as of old and not according to the new rule 3.30 p.m.; also that there would be no sermon and hymns. So I went at 4 o'clock and found after all they had kept to 3.30 p.m. although there was no sermon. I heard the canticles and the anthem at the bottom of the church—Tours in F[8] and "God is our hope"—Greene. It was very fine and not nearly so indistinct as I expected. Things went very well tonight at St. Cuthbert's. Mr. Talbot preached a good sermon on "meditation".

18 Fine day. Martin did not turn up at all today. The boys had no practice tonight. I had tea at Mr. Richardson's. He is getting pedals[9] put to his piano. T.W.B. and I had a short walk in the moonlight at 8.30 p.m. tonight. It was very fine and solemn.

19 Very windy day; the wind is exceedingly strong. Martin has a cold and bad face, poor lad. Rainy night. Went to the Doctor's to look over The Seasons[10] and play a Mendelssohn duet with him.

20 Seasonable weather. Sometimes sunny then suddenly showery. Mr. Tuke called at dinner time to ask me to set music to the "Iron" song. John has taken his music for it away with him. Martin's face is much swollen.

21 Snowy morning. I gave Mr. Gryce the Iron song. It will not be sung, most likely.[11] Frosty night. I soon felt the cold change. It makes me shiver. Got a letter from Fred tonight. The Church temperance society, of which he is secretary, gave a penny reading the other night in the Duke's School.[12] Fred sang a song—Sullivan's "If Doughty Deeds".[13]

1875, January: Aged 16

22 Very fine day. Still frosty, but very cheering. Martin came to church today. Went to Mr. Harrison's as usual. He gave me a guinea tonight for a quarter's teaching.

23 Snow on the ground today. It melted away into mud though, after a bit. I went up to St. Cuthbert's this afternoon and tuned the reed. Steele and Kennedy went to help me. I received a post-card this evening from J. M. Crament[14] containing advertisements of three new pieces of his. Duets at Doctor's tonight, Martin and I.

24 Beautiful day. Mr. Rogers preached this afternoon at the Cathedral. I went home with Mr. Whitehead and had supper tonight and passed a very nice evening.

25 Fine clear weather. I have not heard from John yet. I expected him to write last Wednesday.

26 Rather thick weather. Snow tonight. Miss Brooksbank of the Bailey[15] was married at Bow Church this morning to a Mr. Powell. Took the music-boys tonight.

27 Doctor didn't turn up today, except only to tell me what to do. I went at 12 o'clock to give lessons to the two little Miss Holdens.[16]

28 Rather dull, cold weather. The Doctor sent me to teach the little boys sol-fa-ing, etc. tonight. Received a letter from John at last; he also sent his answers to the paper I set him, with new questions for me to do. He seems to be very busy.

29 Went to Mr. Harrison's tonight as usual.

30 The rehearsals haven't recommenced yet.[17] Piano and harmonium duets with Martin at his house tonight. Coldish weather.

31 Rather fine weather. I played Bach's G minor fugue this afternoon for out-voluntary. The Doctor was pleased and said, "Play it till you get it as steady as a rock." It is a very difficult fugue. The Whiteheads made me go home with them tonight and stay to supper. It appears the St. Cuthbert's organ affair[18] just happened from a mistake or misunderstanding of Mr. Ridley's.

1875, February: Aged 16

February 1 Grand weather. Martin came up tonight and we had some piano duets together.

2 Saw Mr. Bradley of Middlesbro' this morning. He is starting his lessons again. Fine weather. Wrote to W. Biggs [his Alnwick schoolmate] this afternoon, but forgot to post the letter.

3 Fine day. This morning the Doctor said there would be no music-boys and practice this afternoon, that Martin and I might get a holiday! Very good of him. We went to Finchale Abbey at 2 p.m. and enjoyed the outing very much indeed, not getting home till after 6 p.m. It was a most delightful walk. The different scenes kept reminding me of that happy day last Easter when Fred went with us and John joined us after service. Very poor practice at St. Cuthbert's tonight; only three or four girls and one man (Mr. Sewell).

4 Dull, cold day. Wrote nine pages of a letter to John. Will finish it in the morning some time.

5 Piano duets at Doctor's tonight, Martin and I.

6 Gave Artie Harrison his lesson this morning instead of last night. He is getting on exceedingly well. Counterpoint lesson tonight. Harmony for Martin.

7 Doctor got Martin to bring him up to our street, and asked me if I was safe for this afternoon's service. Doctor was not very well I suppose, from what I heard.

8 The Doctor came to practice this morning. Martin and I had a try at the bells this morning. He rings well, but I can't bring a sound out yet. Spent the afternoon across at the Factory chatting with Mr. Harrison. He gave me three or four pencils from Keswick. He gets a lot cheap through a friend, they are slightly spoiled in the varnishing, etc., but are capital pencils. Tonight I did no work. Mr. Downs[19] came in, and I looked through Faust[20] of which he brought a copy. It is very lazy of me. Snow.

9 Shrove Tuesday. Still snow on the ground. Martin got holiday this afternoon. Musical Society started again tonight. Haydn's "Seasons", and Mendelssohn's "St. Paul".

10 Ash Wednesday. Very cold and bleak. We had two Gregorian chants, the Mag. and Nunc [i.e. Magnificat and Nunc Dimittis] this afternoon.

1875, February: Aged 16

11 Weather cold. Mr. Harrison got a new engine yesterday in place of the old one which burst the end out in the late frosty weather.

12 Weather slightly milder today as it is thawing. T.W.B's cheek is very bad at present, he has to put lint, etc. on it and stop indoors. It is an unfortunate thing. I received a short letter from John tonight in which he says he is very poorly and miserable and is disgusted with the town of Bury. All smoke and mist. Poor lad, it is sad for him to be like that so far away from home. I must write to him again as soon as possible. Martin and I had a few duets tonight here.

13 Piano tuned. Wrote to John. Duets with Martin at the Doctor's tonight.

14 After service this morning Mr. Donkin told me I shall finish on the first Sunday in March.[21] He could not get matters arranged with the Doctor. I saw W. Stewart and J. Young this afternoon at the Cathedral. They are now in the Training College. W. Stewart has a very bad cold. I was requested to play the Dead March tonight, for old Mrs. Waite the Sexton's wife, who died today. I have to play at the funeral on Tuesday afternoon. Glorious spring weather all at once.

15 Weather still fine. The boys want to have a paper-chase on Wednesday. The boys are learning St. John's "Passion", Bach. It is nice, but difficult.

16 Fine day. I played the organ at Mrs. Waite's funeral this afternoon, St. Cuthbert's.

17 Weather cloudy and sometimes fine, then rainy. We had the paper-chase. Brutton and I started off at 1.25 p.m. as hares. The hounds gave us ten minutes start. We dodged about Offal wood a good deal, up and down the steep banks, then to Offal village near which place they came up to us and the papers were about done. It was a short chase, not quite an hour, but Brutton chose a capital course and made it very enjoyable. I got on badly with such a weight of papers keeping me back, but Brutton managed well, he is very strong, he had the big bag. I tore my jacket in three places, also my trousers slightly, with scrambling through a hedge. I don't feel so tired tonight as I expected. I have got a bad cough.

18 Weather rather fine. Sam and F.A. came this morning, and we went about the Cathedral. We were disappointed in the Tower. Mr. Hartley gave me the master key that fits the triforium, etc., and I never thought

1875, February: Aged 16

of asking him about the Tower-top door, if it was the same key or not, so when we got right up to the top we were sold, as it required a different key. The two had dinner at the County Hotel and I saw them again at afternoon service, had tea with them, and saw them off at 7.35 p.m. It is to be quite secret.*

19 Martin off yesterday and today with bad cold and a swollen face. Saw C. Vincent again today. Cold, cold weather. A little snow. Mrs. Armes kindly gave me some nice cough medicine tonight.

20 Mendelssohn in B^{b} was done tonight. It is very nice. This is the first time I have heard it done since I came. Very cold weather. Cough still bad, but it is loosening. I think the "Balsam of Aniseed" is a nice softening medicine.

21 Had supper at Mr. Whitehead's tonight.

22 This morning the Doctor kindly told me I might stay away in the afternoon to get a walk. The weather being damp, I spent my time in the Factory, had tea with Mr. Harrison, and then went on to Mr. Whitehead's to have some music with him. However, Mr. Hartley dropped in and had a long chat, so we did not have much music.

23 Spent a little time with Anthony Graham this afternoon. He is not well, having caught a severe cold. He was at home a day or two since and left them all well. He brought me a parcel of Musical Standards from home. It is kind of him to look me up every time he comes. He is a nice fellow. Dull, cold weather.

24 Cold, snowy day. Got up very late and did not get to practice till 9.30 a.m. Had a little music at Mr. Withers' before dinner. He has a nice-toned harmonium, and also has bought an old Broadwood piano which is very decent, though old. I have lent Martin some things to read—"Recreations of a Country Parson"—"Cobbetts Advice" and a number of the Musical Standard which contains a most interesting lecture by Mr. J. Baillie Hamilton[22] on the "Application of Wind to Strings". He is inventing an organ of strings vibrated from wind reeds.

25 Wet, cheerless, weather. Last night someone hit little Kennedy in the eye with a red-hot cinder. He is away today. I made a row about it tonight. It is shameful.

* Could F.A. have been a 'girl-friend' of brother Sam?

1875, February: Aged 16

26 I am getting to be very lazy through retiring and rising late, and wasting time. As this will not pay, I must try and mend. In counterpoint (which I have neglected lately) I will make it a rule to "write at least one canon every day" according to Ouseley's advice. I want to be a good contrapuntist, as I am sure it is the diligent study of Counterpoint only that makes the thoroughly practical musician and composer.

27 Gave Artie Harrison his lesson as usual.

28 The Rev. Pearce preached this afternoon.

March 1 Cold weather; snow. This has been a terribly severe winter. Got a letter from Father this morning enclosing one for Mr. Whitehead. Father wishes to have me home for a week or two as Anthony Graham says I am not well, but I have written an earnest letter trying to stop it, as it will not do just now. I can't be spared away. Spent the evening at Mr. Harrison's.

2 Cold weather. The music-boys didn't get their lessons tonight.

4 Beautiful sunshiny weather. It is quite cheering after the long period of dull, cold weather. It is still cold, of course. I had a short walk in the afternoon. Went to the Doctor's to have a lesson in "The Seasons".

5 Mr. Rogers asked me to take his junior class this morning.

6 Dull, cold weather. Wrote to John, a birthday letter. He will be 21 to-morrow. Fred also wrote and I enclosed his letter. Nice letter from home tonight. Father will not ask leave for me; he will come over at Easter.

7 The wind has changed to the South West today. It is now much warmer. This is John's 21st birthday. It would have been nice to have had him here for the day, but it can't be helped, poor lad. I had dinner and tea with his Father and Mother and spent a very happy day with them. Finished up the time of St. Cuthbert's organ tonight.[23] After the out-voluntary Mr. Ridley came into the organ-loft and spoke very nicely to me, saying he was annoyed things were stopped so suddenly and for such a little cause, and he made me a present of a sovereign. It was very kind of him. He wants to see Father when he comes over.

1875, March: Aged 16

10 Fine day. At morning practice I asked leave for Martin and me to go to the Bülow Recital at Sunderland tonight. The Doctor gave us leave, and as he was going himself, the boys got holiday from afternoon practice. Martin and I went at 3.10 p.m. getting there about 4 p.m. We enjoyed the fine weather, walked about the Park, etc. and saw Charlie Vincent at the station come to meet the Doctor at 6 p.m. The recital began at 8 p.m. We got 3/- tickets, unreserved seats. Charlie and the Doctor came in soon after us and the Doctor, Mr. Vincent and Mr. W. Rae sat one seat in front of us. The recital was magnificent. The programme was almost the same as last year at Newcastle. He was not quite so excited this time. The "Moonlight" was grand.[24] He took the middle movement much slower than I expected; I even thought it a little too slow. The Bach Chromatic Fantasia was magnificently played. The whole performance was a great treat. The Doctor had to hurry off to the 10 p.m. train, and we had supper with the Vincents. They are such a kind, musical family. It was quite enjoyable. Mr. Vincent was exceedingly kind to me and gave me very pressing invitations to go over and try his large organ, etc. We had to hurry off to the train, such a scamper for it. Just caught it nicely and arrived home about a quarter to twelve p.m.

11 Another nice day; this is quite cheering.

12 Billy Martin and I had a chat with Charlie Vincent this morning again. Terrible weather. Rain, sleet, hail, snow, cold, clouds and all sorts of things.

13 Heard from William Biggs tonight. He is getting on well and seems to hold a responsible situation. He has to pay men, keep charge of quarries, etc. etc. He is land-agent. Rides about on a pony—"Toby". He has had two falls lately from Toby. Once he started to teach the animal to stop merely at the word "Wo", and first time he said the word, Toby stopped, having been taught it before, and William came to "Woe" by falling in front. The next fall was a more serious one, he hit his knee so hard against a telegraph post that it knocked him off the pony.

14 Went to Cathedral this morning. Cold, dull weather.

15 Got up at 7 a.m. T.W.B. was good enough to wake me. I have got a good stock of 16 stave music-paper now from Mr. Richardson—three quires.

16 Dull, cold weather. Wrote to Fred, tomorrow being his 21st birthday.

1875, March: Aged 16

17 St. Patrick's Day. The Irish commemorate it by concerts, etc. all over. I went as accompanyist to Darlington with Messrs. Grice, Price and Walker. We had a short practice in the Hall at 4 p.m. where I met the Priors and went home with them to tea. They have the "Dolphin" Inn. Sam came at 7 p.m. and spent the night with us making it very enjoyable indeed for me. The concert went off all right and I got my half-guinea and expenses. Sam stayed all night at the Priors' and we came back to Durham about midnight. I like Darlington. Fred's 21st birthday.

19 I had a play on the partly-finished organ in the Factory tonight; the engine blew. Then I had supper with Mr. and Mrs. Harrison and played on the piano.

20 Weather exceedingly cold. Went to the Doctor's tonight to try over Brahm's Hungarian Dances[25] with him. They are peculiar, but very beautiful. I enjoyed the evening very much.

21 Dull weather.

22 Had a little bit of organ playing in the Factory tonight. The voicing as usual is very sweet.

23 My cold and cough are bad again. I expect it is owing to the Darlington do.

24 Martin and I went to St. Oswald's to have a practice with the choir tonight. I am to play on Sundays and Martin Wednesdays and Fridays. Dr. Dykes is very ill and is going to have six months rest. He has gone to London to consult the doctors. I hope the change will put him right, everybody misses his face.

25 Father came at about 3 o'clock this afternoon. He went across and saw Mr. Harrison at the Factory and came along in time to hear the Selection from St. John's Account of the Passion—Bach. It went very well. The choruses were sublime, more stirring than any I have heard before I almost think. Hyde sang a lovely solo, "I follow Thee, Also". Father was much pleased with the Passion. Father and I had tea with the Whiteheads. Poor John is in very low spirits I hear. He mopes about and has not the heart for study. I am very sorry for him.

26 ***Good Friday***. Beautiful, sunny day.

1875, March: Aged 16

27 Fine day, but very windy. Father and I chose the desk for me to give Fred. It is a very nice one made of rosewood, cost one sovereign. Father and I went to dinner with the Doctor, and he was in a capital humour, making it a very enjoyable visit. Father went away at 3 p.m. to Middlesbro'. Mr. James Lawson of Coxhoe[26] was in today.

28 *Easter Day*. I played at St. Oswald's.

29 Father came here this afternoon and went home at half-past four.

April 5 I asked the Doctor today if he would allow me to teach Mr. Withers the piano. He was quite willing and glad that I should do so.

6 I gave Mr. Withers his first lesson this afternoon. He wishes me to spend one evening per week over oratorios with him—terms being two guineas a quarter for all.

7 Had a short oratorio practice with Mr. Withers tonight. Then I went to the Doctor's for a lesson in the Seasons.

8 Rainy, stormy day.

9 This afternoon I saw Miss Morrell at the Cathedral. Tonight at St. Oswald's choir-practice they tried for the first time some new chants out of Hopkins' collection of "Single chants for unison use with additional harmonies for the Organ". They are very good indeed. Mr. Rogers kindly gave me a copy when I was at his house last week. The Rev. Mr. Dunn was at church and practice. He is Dr. Dykes' deputy.

10 Mr. Donkin wants me to teach his son on the organ. I will have to see about it.

11 The Hopkins Chants were first used today at St. Oswald's.

12 Fine day.

13 Very fine cheering weather. I have made up my mind to do a double counterpoint daily as well as a canon.

14 Had a good long game at cricket with Martin till 12, then we were umpires in the boys' game. Very beautiful weather. Mr. Harrison tells

1875, April: Aged 16

me that Artie is ill, poor little fellow. Tried over the Mendelssohn and Brahms duets again with the Doctor tonight.

17 Nice warm weather. Gave W. Donkin his first organ lesson today. The Doctor kindly allows me to have pupils, so long as I don't shirk my work for him.

18 Nice day.

19 Got up rather earlier, and had a short walk. I wish I were an early riser. Martin and I played at cricket with the boys today. Warm weather.

20 Mrs. Lawson was very poorly tonight. I am afraid she is over-worked. Hot weather. Martin's birthday. He is 18 years old.

22 Weather rather cold, but mostly fine. Mr. Lawson's birthday.

23 Cold weather.

Aged 17

24 My birthday. I am 17 years old. This morning's post I received a little box from home containing three nice letters from Father, Mother and Fred, a gold pin from Father and Mother and a tie from Fred. It is very kind of them to remember unworthy me so affectionately. Got a little birthday letter from Sam in the afternoon.

25 Nice weather.

28 Mr. Withers and I had a walk to Bear Park before breakfast. Last night, at W's suggestion, I hung some string out of the window, having one end tied to my wrist. But with shifting about through the night it got too high for Mr. Withers to reach. However, with having such eager expectations, I woke very early.

29 Grammar School Sports. I did not go. Fair, warm weather.

30 Mr. Withers and I started at 6.15 a.m. and went by Framwellgate Moor to Finchale Abbey. Got there about 7.30 a.m.; had some nice new milk and bun, and came back by Frankland. It was a splendid walk, glorious weather. How I did enjoy it! Got in to practice at 9.15 a.m.

May 1 At 5 this morning I was wakened capitally by the string; and when I hauled in there was a piece of paper tied to the end bearing these

1875, May: Aged 17

words, "Well pulled by bonny May Gosling"! I don't know who did it. Mr. Withers and everybody deny it. Cold, dull day.

2 Mr. Withers and I had a good long walk before breakfast. We went to Rilly paper mill and round by Ushaw College, eight or nine miles.

4 Miscellaneous concert of the Musical Society tonight. Everything went well, especially Pierson's Roman Dirge.[27] The Doctor and I played Nocturne and Scherzo from Mendelssohn's Midsummernight's Dream, also three of Brahm's Hungarian Dances.

6 Martin and I went with St. Oswald's choir to Finchale this afternoon. The brake started a little after 2 p.m. and it rained hard when we were going, but when we got there the weather brightened up till it was glorious. Tea at 5 p.m., then a short service in the ruins, which was very nice and impressive, and we started home about 6 p.m. and got in in good time for evening service.

7 Tonight the Doctor tried over the harmonium parts of The Seasons and I played the piano.

9 Nice day, though occasionally wet looking.

11 Got up late.

13 Warm weather. Mr. Hiller tuned the piano this afternoon.

15 I went with Mr. Richardson to Towlaw[28] today. We went in a two-wheeler, starting about 8 a.m. Went round by Witton-Gilbert to call at a friend's of the Richardson's,[29] the Brandon's. Poor Mr. Brandon was to have gone with us today, but he died on Thursday or Friday. Very sad. The country from Witton-Gilbert was really splendid. I could hardly believe there was such grand scenery in the county of Durham. That very great valley through which the Derness flows was glorious. The Wooley men had a rehearsal at 10.30 a.m. at the Daglish's, where we got dinner. Then we walked over to Towlaw. I liked the bandsmen well, they seemed all so respectable and goodnatured. The contest began about 12 p.m. and ended about 6 p.m. Four bands played two pieces each. The Felling Band got first prize, Wooley (Mr. Richardson's) second prize, Sunniside third and Skelton played abominably. The judge was very pleased with Mr. Richardson's arrangement from Spohr's "Faust". It was very nice. We had tea at Mr. Campbell's, Towlaw, and after a

1875, May: Aged 17

very fine drive the same way back we got home about 10 p.m. I did not give W. Donkin his organ lesson today.

16 Whitsunday.

19 Counterpoint lesson.

20 Tonight I gave Miss Earle her first piano lesson. Terms are to be one guinea per quarter.

21 Short counterpoint lesson. As there was nearly one year's work to examine, the Doctor could only do a little of it on Wednesday night and tonight.

22 Fine weather, but windy. John Biggs has come home from his long voyage and has grown all ways, so Mother says. Mr. Withers went with me to St. Oswald's tonight, and we had a little music afterwards.

23 ***Trinity Sunday.***

28 Confirmation at St. Nicholas' today. T.W.B. was confirmed, so was Hyde.

June 3 The weather is very hot at present.

5 I gave Donkin a short lesson today as I couldn't get it in in the afternoon and only about half-an-hour at night.

7 Rehearsal at the Town Hall tonight for tomorrow night.

8 The "Seasons"—Haydn, went very fairly. Doctor played the harmonium and conducted, Martin and I were at the piano. I found that I had entered into the music last night so, I could not go at it again tonight with the same vigour. I must use discretion another time.

9 Some of the First Royal Dragoons came here today on their way south. The uniform looked nice—red with yellow stripes, brass helmets. The horses seemed fine animals.

10 Miss Earle did not get her lesson tonight as I had to go to St. Oswald's. I am to go on Monday instead.

9. St Nicholas Church, Durham

1875, June: Aged 17

11 Cold, showery weather.

14 Miss Earle got her lesson tonight instead of last Friday. After the lesson I went and had a game at chess and draughts with Mr. Withers with whom I have supped, slept and breakfasted since Saturday night.

19 Artie Harrison did not have his lesson this morning. A baby brother born.[30]

21 No lessons with Mr. Withers till he comes back. He goes away tomorrow morning.

24 Miss Earle did not have her lesson tonight as I went to St. Oswald's.

27 Mrs. Armes was at St. Oswald's this morning and after service she invited me to dinner and I was very pleased. Wet day.

28 Gave Miss Earle her lesson tonight instead of Friday last. Doctor gone for his month's holiday. He and Mrs. Armes go first to Windermere, then France, Switzerland and Italy.

29 Damp, raw weather. I have begun learning "Musikography" by J. Gompertz Montefiore.[31]

July 1 Miss Earle did not get her lesson tonight.

2 Wet afternoon. Got organ and piano catalogues from Novello's this morning. They require some satisfactory proof of my being a bona-fide teacher of music, so I must try and get some friends to sign their names.

3 Mr. Rogers kindly wrote on Novello's circular for me.

5 John came this morning at 5.30 a.m. He looks exceedingly well, fat and broad shouldered. Two friends, George and John Openshaw, came with him. We all had breakfast at the Whiteheads', then a walk before practice. After service I borrowed the Doctor's volume of Mendelssohn Overtures (4 hand) etc. and we played till dinner. After dinner we went to the Regatta. Miss Earle is away till Friday so she could not have had her lesson tonight.

126 1875 May/June

23 - Trinity Sunday.

28 - Confirmation at St. Nicholas' today. T. W. B was confirmed, so was Hyde.

June 3rd - The weather is very hot at present.

5th - I gave Donkin a short lesson today as I couldn't get in the afternoon & only about ½ hr at night.

7th - Rehearsal at the Town Hall tonight for tomorrow night.

8th - The "Seasons" (Haydn) went very fairly. Dr. played the harmonium & conducted. Martin & I were at the Piano. I found that I had entered into the music last night so I ~~could~~ could not go at it again tonight with the same vigour. I must use discretion another time.

9th - Some of the 1st Royal Dragoons came here today on their way South. The uniform looked nice, red with yellow stripes, brass helmets. The horses seemed fine animals.

10th - Miss Earle did not get her lesson tonight as I had to go to St. Oswald's. I ~~will~~ am to go on Monday instead.

11 - Cold showery weather.

14 - Miss Earle got her lesson tonight instead of last Friday. After the lesson I went & had a game at chess & drafts with Mr. Withers with whom I have supped, slept & breakfasted since Saturday night.

15 - Mr. Withers' father-in-law came tonight.

19 - Artie H. did not learn his lesson this morning. A baby brother born.

21 - No lessons with Mr. Withers till he comes back. He goes away tomorrow morn.

24 - Miss Earle did not have her lesson tonight as I went to St Oswald's.

27 - Mr. Armes was at St Oswald's this morning and after service he invited me to dinner and I was very pleased. Wet day

10. Page from end of Diary (1875)

1875, July: Aged 17

6 John and his friends went to Finchale this afternoon. Very hot weather.

7 The Precentor took the boys to Redcar. Mr. Lawson, John and Martin went as well. Hot day.

8 The Openshaws went away this morning.

10 Wind, and occasional rain. John took me with him last night to Mr. Salkeld's.

11 Mr. Withers has come home and brought his bride.

12 They are commencing whitewashing and painting the Song-School. Father and Mother have gone to Scotland today. I hope they will thoroughly enjoy their trip. I have had a lot of toothache lately owing to several decaying teeth. I have got some india rubber for them.

August 3 Met Mr. Brewis of Morpeth at Mr. Harrison's tonight. I like him very much.

4 The funeral of poor little Dobson took place this afternoon. Four boys went to be pallbearers. A special hymn and the Dead March were done at the Cathedral in the afternoon. The loss of little Dobbie has been a great distress to us all. I went to Vincent's this afternoon, saw Mr. V's large organ (Willis), played duets at night till 1.30 a.m.!

5 Got home from Sunderland at 9.30 a.m. After morning service the boys and we went to Brancepeth bazaar at the Dean's expense and spent a pleasant day.

7 Doctor came to church this morning after his holiday. I think he looks better and brighter. Duets with him tonight. Doctor very kindly gave me Five Pounds to take home with me as a reward for doing the work for him! Very generous indeed of him. I go home on Monday morning—August 9th.

[*Completion of apprenticeship. End of Diary.*]

T. H. Collinson

From the Churchwardens of
St. Oswald's, Durham in
recognition of the valuable services
he rendered to that Church,
as Organist, during the last
illness of the Rev. J. B. Dykes Mus Doc

Durham

October 31. 1877

11. Inscription to T. H. C. on fly-leaf of bound presentation volume of music

L'ENVOI

With the completion of Thomas Henry Collinson's time as an apprentice, the diary comes to its natural end—perhaps a little abruptly, as I said in the Introduction! He kept no further diary until well into his old age. It is possible however to reconstruct the main events of his career in the period immediately following, partly from documentary and printed sources, and partly from what he, my father, told me in later life.

His apprenticeship accomplished and behind him, the time had arrived for him to decide what to do next. An apprenticeship to a cathedral organist led naturally to a like musical career in the service of the Church. One need hardly say that Philip Armes wished for nothing better than to see his pupil secure an appointment commensurate with his musical talents, and he rated these highly. It should, he adjudged, be a cathedral appointment and not an ordinary church organistship.

A few months later, in 1876, it happened that the sub-organistship of St Paul's Cathedral, London became vacant.[1] There was, too, another prospective post in the offing. In 1874, a year before the completion of his apprenticeship, the foundation stone had been laid of a new cathedral in Edinburgh, to be named St Mary's. The appointment of an organist and choirmaster of the new foundation would almost certainly be made within a year or two.

Dr Armes offered his pupil the choice of his recommendation and sponsorship for either of these appointments. He chose to wait and try for the new cathedral appointment when it should mature, rather than for the assistant organistship of St Paul's Cathedral, even with the expectation of succession to the organistship in due course. The reason for his decision, it may be said, was typical of him. It was, as he declared to me in later life, that the building up of a musical tradition from the very first beginnings in a new cathedral would present not only the greater challenge but 'the greater opportunity for service' (his own words). It cannot be denied that it

[1] The post of sub-organistship of St Paul's Cathedral became vacant on the death of its holder, George Cooper, Jr, who had succeeded to the office on the death of his father, George Cooper, Sen. The Organist of St Paul's at that time was John Stainer, later to become Sir John Stainer, Professor of Music at Oxford. He is probably best known as the composer of the one-time popular oratorio, 'The Crucifixion'. Cf. West, op. cit.

was a bold decision, for there could be no knowing but that, having declined the chance of the first appointment, the second might also elude him.

Meanwhile, in the same year of 1876, Dr J. B. Dykes died. In consequence, the organistship of St Oswald's Church, Durham became vacant. Thomas Henry Collinson had already become assistant organist to Dr Dykes (who acted as his own organist) and the post was offered to him. He accepted, on the understanding that the appointment could only be a temporary one, of fairly short duration.

To put the period of waiting to good use he commenced to study for the degree of MusBac at Oxford. For his 'exercise' for the degree he composed a setting for choir and orchestra of the 65th Psalm, 'Thou O God art praised in Sion'. In 1897, at the age of eighteen, he took the degree. Of his musical setting of the Psalm, Sir F. A. G. Ouseley, Professor of Music at Oxford, wrote, 'I am very glad to say that your admirable exercise has given very great satisfaction to myself and my coadjutors'.[1]

In the year following, the post matured for which he had waited, and he duly applied for it. His application was successful; on 24 September 1878, at the age of twenty, he was appointed Organist and Master of the Choristers of St Mary's Cathedral Edinburgh,[2] an office he was to hold for the next fifty years.[3]

[1] Cf. biographical article, unsigned, *The Musical Times* (1 April 1908).
[2] That is, the Episcopal cathedral; there is now a Roman Catholic cathedral of the same name in Edinburgh.
[3] Cf. 'A Centenary of Music at St Mary's Cathedral and the Man who inspired it', Janet Joy Foster, *The Scottish Tatler* (June 1979).

12. St Mary's Cathedral, Edinburgh, by Charles Napier, RSW.

THE REST OF THE STORY IN BRIEF

Thomas Henry Collinson, MusBac Oxon; organist and choirmaster of St Mary's Cathedral Edinburgh; 1878–1928.
Appointed conductor of the Edinburgh Choral Union (subsequently Edinburgh Royal Choral Union) 1883–1914.
Among the first performances in Scotland conducted by him in this capacity were:

Gounod; *Redemption, 1883*
Dvorak; *Stabat Mater, 1886*
Elgar; *Dream of Gerontius, 1903*
Parry; *Voces Clamanticus, 1904*
J. S. Bach; *Mass in B Minor, 1907*

Performance as solo pianist with the Edinburgh Choral Union of Beethoven's Choral Fantasia; conducted by Sir August Manns, 1883.
Appointed lecturer in music to the Theological College of the Episcopal Church, 1880.
Marriage to Miss Annie Wyness Scott, Edinburgh, 6 January 1891.
Invitation by Edinburgh University to become Organist to the University, which post he accepted, 1898.
Appointed conductor of the Edinburgh Amateur Orchestral Society, 1900–1924.
Degree of FRCO conferred—*honoris causa,* 1904.
Gave organ recital at opening of the Usher Hall, Edinburgh, 1914.
Intimation from Edinburgh University of wish to confer upon him the degree of DMus Edin, 7 December 1927.
At Edinburgh, 17 February 1928, death of Thomas Henry Collinson, aged seventy.
Degree of DMus Edin conferred posthumously by Edinburgh University.

NOTES ON DIARY

ABBREVIATIONS

Scholes	*Oxford Companion to Music,* edited by Percy A. Scholes, fourth edition (Oxford 1942).
Grove	*Grove's Dictionary of Music & Musicians,* fourth edition, edited by H. C. Colles (London 1940).
	The New Grove: Ed. Stanley Sadie, 1980.
Muirhead	*England,* in Blue Guides series, Finlay Muirhead (London 1930).
Murray	*Handbook for Travellers in Durham and Northumberland,* John Murray (London 1864).
Stranks	*Durham Cathedral,* The Venerable C. J. Stranks, Pitkin series of Pictorial Guides.
Bartholomew	*Survey Gazetteer of the British Isles,* J. G. Bartholomew (London 1904).
Encyclo. Brit.	*The Encyclopaedia Britannica,* fourteenth edition (London & New York, 1929, 1930).
West	*Cathedral Organists, John E. West* (London 1899).
Thomson	*The International Cyclopedia of Music and Musicians,* edited by Oscar Thomson (Binghampton N.Y., and London, 1938, 1942).
Mee	*Durham,* Arthur Mee, revised B. Berryman, The King's England series (London 1964).
Rushford	*In and Around Durham,* Frank H. Rushford (Durham 1946).

REFERENCES

Durham Cathedral (leaflet published by): *Bells Past and Present in Durham Cathedral.* N.d.

The Durham Advertiser, excerpts from 1871–1876.

The Durham Directory and Almanack, 1876, 1878, 1895.

Elvin, Lawrence, *The Harrison Story*; Harrison & Harrison, organbuilders, Durham. Pub. author, Lincoln 1973.

Walker, George, *A Sketch of Durham, 1885*; republished 1972. E. J. Morton, Didsbury.

Welldon, J. E. C. and Wall, James, *The Story of Durham Cathedral* 1930, republished by Raphael Tuck & Sons Ltd, 1935.

The Musical Times; April 1, 1908. Mr. T H Collinson (writer un-named).

NOTES

Many of the persons who cross the pages of the diary appear as no more than names, often only as initials. Diligent research might possibly bring to light a few details of who they were and what they did. Such, however, to my mind, is the graphic quality of the writing that few names appear of which the owners do not at once spring to life as real people, however brief their mention. In many such cases therefore I feel that no harm will be done in leaving things as they are.

F.C.

1871

1. 5.10.1871. There were two services at the Cathedral, morning service (Matins) at 10 a.m. and evening service (Evensong) at 4 p.m. (3.30 p.m. from Oct. 1874).
2. 6.10.71. The Doctor, Dr Philip Armes.
3. 6.10.71. The prelude and fugue can be identified from subsequent entries as the first of J. S. Bach's Forty-Eight Preludes and Fugues, *The well-tempered Clavier.*
4. 7.10.71. John Whitehead, the senior of the three apprentices. He evidently belonged to Durham, as the diary refers to his father's garden allotment being situated there (cf. p. 43, 10 May 1873).
5. 7.10.71. St Nicholas Church, situated in the Market Place; known as 'The Market Church'. The present church is of nineteenth-century date, erected on the site of the twelfth-century church built by Bishop Flambard (Mee).
6. 7.10.71. German pedals; these were organ pedals of an early type, usually of only one octave in compass. They did not operate pipes of their own, but only drew down the corresponding keys on the manual (Grove).
7. 7.10.71. The Church of St Nicholas, see above.
8. 8.10.71. Durham Cathedral has a peal of ten bells. There were eight in T.H.C's day.
9. 8.10.71. The Church of St Oswald is of 11th-12th century date (Rushford) (late 12-15th century (Muirhead)). It is described by Mee as 'The Mother Church of Durham'. The vicar at the time of the diary was the well-known composer of hymn tunes, Dr J. B. Dykes (cf. Introduction). T.H.C. became assistant organist to Dr Dykes during his apprenticeship, and was appointed organist as his successor at St Oswalds on the death of Dr Dykes in 1876, a post he held for two years, prior to his Edinburgh Cathedral appointment in 1878 (cf. 'L'Envoi').
10. 8.10.71. Richard was a cousin, or probably a step cousin, of T.H.C. He was his senior by eleven years. The photograph, plate 5, on a metal plate, probably a kind of Daguerreotype, shows T.H.C. standing with Richard seated. Richard is holding a Northumbrian bagpipe. The photograph is contemporary with the date of its mention in the diary and shows T.H.C. at the age of thirteen.

11. 8.10.71. T.H.C. lodged with the Lawsons in Durham. The Durham Directory and Almanack of 1876 lists Thomas Lawson, teacher, as living at 3 Cross Street, Durham. Cross Street has since been merged with Hawthorn Terrace, where is situated the organ factory of Messrs Harrison & Harrison which figures so often in the diary. It is possible that Thomas Lawson may have been a friend of Thomas Collinson senior, who was headmaster of the Duke's School, Alnwick; or at least the shared profession of teaching may have established the point of contact. The Durham Directory also gives a William Lawson 'formerly of Durham' as the author of textbooks on geography, and states that he was Tutor of St Mark's College (whereabouts not known). He died on 18 May 1895. The Durham Directory states that in 1874 at No. 2 Cross Street, i.e. next door to the Lawsons, there lived T. Webb, organ builder—probably one of the staff of the organ factory along the street.
12. 9.10.71. The Dean of Durham at that time was the Very Revd William Charles Lake.
13. 9.10.71. i.e. practising on the organ.
14. 10.10.71. Turner's Diorama; a kind of static peep-show.
15. 13.10.71. Nevil's Cross (*recte*, Neville's Cross); the remains of a stone cross 1 mile SW of Durham. It was formerly encircled by statues of the four evangelists and surmounted by a crucifix, but these were wantonly destroyed in 1589, only the lower part of the shaft and the stone steps of the pedestal remaining. The Cross celebrates the battle between the Scots under King David II, son of Robert the Bruce, and the English under Lords Neville and Percy, supported by the Archbishop of York and the Bishops of Durham, Lincoln and Carlisle. The battle, fought on 17 October 1346, resulted in a disastrous defeat for the Scots, in which their king, David II was taken prisoner. The actual scene of the battle was Red Hills, on the west of the city (Muirhead; Murray).
16. 14.10.71. The Cathedral Library contains relics of Saint Cuthbert, which were transferred first from Lindisfarne to Chester-le-Street in 883, and thence to Durham in 995 (Muirhead).
17. 14.10.71. Prebends' Bridge; erected by the Dean & Chapter in 1772 to replace a footbridge upstream carried away by the river in 1770 (Mee). It was while standing on Prebends' Bridge that Sir Walter Scott composed the lines in Harold the Dauntless (Canto Third)—

    Grey Towers of Durham . . .
    Yet well I love thy mixed and massive piles,
      Half church of God, half castle 'gainst the Scot,
    And long to roam these venerable aisles—
      With records stored of deeds long since forgot.

    The lines are inscribed on a tablet fixed in the stonework of the approach to the bridge from the west side of the river.
18. 15.10.71. Anthony Graham was in due time to become an architect.
19. 17.10.71. John Baptist Cramer, b. Mannheim 1771; d. London 1858. His pianoforte studies were highly thought of in the nineteenth century and are still in use. Beethoven thought highly of his playing (Scholes).
20. 22.10.71. Bearpark (the name is said to be a corruption of Bearepaire) is a park to the NW of Durham. In it is a moss-grown gabled fragment which is all that remains of the country palace of the Priors of Durham. It is one of the beauty spots of Durham (Murray).
21. 24.10.71. 'Dinner', in northern parlance, means lunch; T.H.C's piano practice was therefore completed during the morning.
22. 29.10.71. Mr Gryce; one of the lay-clerks (i.e. choir men) at Durham Cathedral.
23. 1.11.71. 'Organ in the afternoon'; at this period the evening service seems to have been sung without organ accompaniment.
24. 10.11.71. Ellingham Hall is a country seat about eight miles north of Alnwick. Mr Thorpe was evidently a friend of T.H.C's father; possibly one of the governors of the Duke's School.

25. 16.11.71. St Cuthbert's Church is in North Road, Durham; built in 1862 in French style architecture.
26. 16.11.71. The river is the River Wear which flows round the city of Durham on three sides, almost surrounding it.

1872

1. 14.1.72. The illness was measles; the information is added by T.H.C. in a later handwriting.
2. 14.1.72. The duties of organist and choirmaster at St Cuthbert's Church seem to have been undertaken by the music apprentices of the Cathedral under the supervision of Dr Armes.
3. 15.1.72. William ('Billy') Martin was the other of the three apprentices under the tutelege of Dr Armes. Martin's Christian name only occurs once throughout the diary (in the form 'Billy') viz. on 12 Mar. 1875.
4. 16.1.72. Crossgate Road and district lies across the river to the NW of the peninsula.
5. 18.1.72. *The Village Organist,* a collection of pieces for the organ; edited by John (later Sir John) Stainer.
6. 18.1.72. Massaniello (*recte,* Masaniello) also known as *The Dumb Girl of Portici*; opera by Daniel F. E. Auber, b. Caen 1782, d. Paris 1871 (Scholes). The copy in question was probably either a vocal score of the opera, or an arrangement of the Overture for pianoforte.
7. 18.1.72. *Zauberflöte,* the opera by Mozart. A copy of the vocal score (now in my possession) was given to T.H.C. by Dr Armes. F.C.
8. 20.1.72. *As pants the hart for cooling streams,* anthem by Louis Spohr, b. Brunswick 1784, d. Cassel 1859 (Scholes).
9. 20.1.72. Nicholson and Macbeth were choirboys at the Cathedral. Nicholson became a captain in the merchant navy.
10. 20.1.72. Samuel Webbe; there were two composers of that name, father and son. (1) b. London 1740, d. London 1816; (2) b. London 1770, d. Liverpool 1843. They were chiefly renowned for the composition of glees and catches, but also composed church music, principally anthems (Scholes). These anthems were printed in open score, with a separate stave to each voice, each stave bearing its appropriate clef, i.e. soprano (C) clef, treble clef, alto and tenor (C) clefs, and bass clef. These formed a taxing exercise in reading the clefs. F.C.
11. 23.1.72. Mimic opera; a clear definition of the term cannot be found. Possibly the opera was performed by marionettes with the music sung by a concealed cast of singers with accompaniment by pianoforte or small orchestra, as was commonly done in those days. The voices and orchestra are now provided by gramophone records or tape recordings. Cf. Grove, *Marionette Theatre.*
12. 25.1.72. The diary does not identify the composer; Auber, Weber, Lizst, Chopin and Heller have all composed examples of the Tarantella (Scholes).
13. 25.1.72. Stephen Heller, b. Budapest 1814, d. Paris 1888; composed many short pieces for the pianoforte, graceful in style and not difficult to play. He was a friend of Chopin, Lizst, Berlioz and Schumann (Scholes).
14. 29.1.72. Rink (*recte,* Rinck). Johann C. H., b. Thuringia 1770, d. Darmstadt 1846; composer of much organ music, some of which is still played (Scholes). His best known work is his *Practical Organ School* (Grove).
15. 31.1.72. The Kyrie referred to was evidently the composition of T.H.C. It has not survived.
16. 1.2.72. The two-headed nightingale and the dwarf. The dwarf may possibly be the figure carved in stone of a small man seated cross-legged with his hands clasped on top of his

head. The figure is to be found on the second boss away from the main altar, above the credence table in the Sanctuary. Alternatively, but not so likely, the dwarf may refer to the small square stone marking the grave in the Cathedral of the Polish Count Boruwlaski, a well-known figure in Durham in the first half of the nineteenth century. He was only three feet three inches in height, though otherwise well-proportioned. The stone is let into the floor at the west end of the north aisle and bears the initials J.B. and a tiny cross (Mee). The Count was exiled from Poland for political offences, and made his home in Durham. He was an accomplished musician and a popular figure in the great houses of the city and county. His house, since demolished, stood near the east end of Prebends' Bridge, at the head of the city peninsula, below the Cathedral. He died at the age of ninety-eight in 1837—thirty-four years before the commencement of T.H.C's diary. There is a brass memorial tablet to the Count in the church of St Mary-the-less in the South Bailey, and a life-sized portrait of him by Hastings in the lobby of the Town Hall. The *two-headed nightingale* cannot be identified by the present Cathedral authorities, and it seems to be an object of Cathedral lore since become lost or forgotten.

17. 4.2.72. The Training College [for school-teachers] for the parcel from Alnwick; evidently a private means of such transportation by Thomas Collinson senior. As a headmaster in the neighbouring county he would doubtless be well-known at the Durham T.C.

18. 13.2.72. Writing chants; i.e. copying out Anglican chants to which the Psalms are sung in prose form in the Church of England service.

19. 24.2.72. i.e. copied out the chants as above.

20. 27.2.72. 'Upwards of 8000 people in the Cathedral at morning service'. This is a palpable over-estimate; the Cathedral seats about 2000 maximum. 800 people would be nearer the mark. (Information from R. Wright, Durham.)

21. 6.3.72. 'Played the chants at service'; i.e. accompanied on the organ the singing of the Psalms by the choir at service at the Cathedral. It may be of interest to note that T.H.C. was playing the organ at services in the cathedral at the age of thirteen.

22. 12.3.72. Red Hills; high broken ground rising from the River Wear on the west of the city; the site of contact between the Scots and English armies at the battle of Neville's Cross (Murray).

23. 15.3.72. The 'cello part of these sonatas for pianoforte and violoncello would doubtless be played on the harmonium at their music-making at Dr Armes' house.

24. 16.3.72. T. W. Brewis ('T.W.B.') was a close friend of T.H.C. at Durham. He must either have lived in the same lodgings or had access to them at any hour of the day or night, for he used to waken T.H.C. at a very early hour of the morning to go for a walk etc. Perhaps people left their front-doors unlocked in those days.

25. 23.3.72. i.e. the 'out-voluntary' after the Cathedral service. He adds in later writing the title of the piece—*Lead on, lead on* [*in majesty*].

26. 25.3.72. The Factory Choral practice; this would seem to refer to a choral society or group formed by the personnel of one or more of the factories in Durham. It could not have included the organ factory of Harrison & Harrison, as T. H. Harrison, founder of the firm, only came to Durham from Rochdale in the summer of 1872.

27. 4.4.72. 'Scraping the nave'; the interior walls of the Cathedral were in earlier times coated with plaster and whitewash. This was removed between the years 1872 and 1876 by the direction of Sir Gilbert Scott, the well-known architect, who at the same time erected the present marble and alabaster screen at the entrance to the choir from the nave, besides other work (Strank). The *Durham Advertiser* of 29 March 1872 reports that 'a Mr Joseph Taylor has received the contract for removing the colour on the walls and pillars of the Cathedral nave. Colour had already been removed from the North Aisle and Nine Altars; Choir and other portions are still to be treated.'

28. 8.4.72. These refer to pianoforte sonatas by these composers.

29. 9.4.72. The *Son and Stranger*; the English title of Mendelssohn's one-act singspiel, *Helmkehr aus der Fremde*.

30. 9.4.72. The nineteenth of Bach's *48*, in A major.
31. 9.4.72. The twentieth of Bach's *48* in A minor; a very long and difficult fugue.
32. 9.4.72. The choruses of Handel's choral works were transcribed for organ by William Thomas Best, b. Carlisle 1826, d. Liverpool 1897. Best was organist of St George's Hall, Liverpool (Grove).
33. 11.4.72. T.H.C. had evidently played the pianoforte at the performance of the singspiel.
34. 15.4.72. The Revd Minor Canon Edward Greatorex, MA was the Precentor of Durham at that date. The Durham Directory and Almanac of 1872 states that he was the son of Dr Thomas Greatorex, one-time organist of Westminster Abbey. In 1872, he accepted the living of Croxdale, an ecclesiastical district 3 miles south of Durham city. He lived till 1901. 'Greatorex's' in the diary entry, presumably means the home of the Greatorex family in Durham. cf. later refs.
35. 26.4.72. *Holy Jesu*; possibly the hymn tune to *Hear us Holy Jesu* (Hymns Ancient & Modern Nos. 466 and 467). Dr J. B. Dykes composed one of the four tunes for the hymn appearing in this collection. It is not by any means one of his best tunes. F.C.
36. 27.4.72. 'Harmonised . . . Nicene Creed'—i.e. arranged harmonies to accompany the *Nicene Creed* to be sung by the choir at St Oswald's Church the following morning.
37. 1.5.72. 'I expect this is the last time.' This is a curious statement. In actual fact T.H.C. was to be closely associated with St Oswald's Church during his apprenticeship, and afterwards became the official organist of that church. cf. 31/1/75.
38. 6.5.72. King in F, i.e. music for the morning service as composed in the key of F by Charles King (1687–1748) Master of the Choristers, St Paul's Cathedral, London; composer of church services and anthems (Scholes).
39. 6.5.72. Second fugue, Bach, second part; Bach's 48 Preludes and Fugues consists of two parts, each containing 24 preludes and fugues, one in each key of the scale. The fugue here referred to was the second fugue in Part II, in C minor.
40. 6.5.72. Mr Greatorex's lecture; cf. 15/4/72. His name also occurs in connection with the photographing of the cast of *The Son and Stranger* (15 Apr. 1872). John Whitehead, the senior apprentice, evidently played the musical illustrations to the Greatorex lecture on the pianoforte. cf. Note 68. 4/9/72.
41. 6.5.72. *The Carman's Whistle*; (*a*) a ballad with its tune, first published in 1592. Cf. William Chappell, *Popular Music of the Olden Time* (London 1855–9). (*b*) a piece for the harpsichord by William Byrd (b. *c.*1542) based on the tune of the ballad. This appears in the Fitzwilliam and Lady Neville's Virginal Books.
42. 7.5.72. Charles Morrell; a former Alnwick schoolmate.
43. 25.5.72. i.e. the seventh fugue in the second book of the *48*; in E flat major.
44. 29.5.72. Royal Oak Day. The English victory over the Scots at the Battle of Red Hills, or Neville's Cross, is celebrated annually by the singing of three anthems from the top of the central tower of the Cathedral on the twenty-ninth of May. Royal Oak Day has nothing to do with this battle, but celebrates the escape of King Charles II by hiding in an oak tree, after his defeat at Worcester, and his subsequent restoration to the throne. At Durham the celebration of the two events was conveniently merged in the same day of the year, 29 May, and now on the nearest Saturday to this date. cf. 29/5/73.
45. 6.6.72. The 'swell to great coupler'; this is the mechanism, controlled by an organ stop, which connects the notes (and sometimes the actual keys) of the 'swell organ' manual or keyboard to the corresponding notes or keys of the 'great organ' on the keyboard below.
46. 8.6.72. Johann N. Hummel; b, Bratislavia 1778, d. Weimar 1837; a pupil of Mozart and friend of Beethoven; composed much pianoforte and other music (Scholes).
47. 12.6.72. Finchale Abbey (properly, *Priory*); founded as a cell to Durham Priory in 1196, on the site of the Hermitage of St Godric (Muirhead).
48. 12.6.72. Kepier (or Kepyer) Wood; a beauty spot two miles to the north of the city, abounding in wild flowers, where the River Wear flows among large moss-grown stones through a deep rocky ravine (Murray).

49. 12.6.72. Framwellgate Moor; an open moorland immediately to the north of the city, bordering on the suburb of Framwellgate (Muirhead).

50. 14.6.72. The Durham Regatta; a two-day regatta on the River Wear, held annually during the third week in June. The Durham Miners' Gala (15 June 1872), is now held annually in July.

51. 17.6.72. The Brownie (*recte*, Browney or Bruné) a stream situated in the NW of Durham, crossed by the ancient 'Stone Bridge'. T.H.C.'s bathe and walk mentioned in the diary must have taken place in the morning, before setting out on his visit home to Alnwick.

52. 17.6.72. Alnmouth; a sea-coast resort with harbour at the mouth of the River Aln; 3 miles SE of Alnwick.

53. 21.6.72. Hulne Abbey; the ruins of an ancient priory in Hulne Park, 3 miles NE of Alnwick; founded 1240; possibly the earliest example of a Carmelite friary in England (Muirhead).

54. 21.6.72. Militia Review; Thomas Collinson senior was an officer of the Northumberland Militia, Artillery. Cf. plate 2.

55. 22.6.72. Charles Moore; T.H.C's first organ teacher at Alnwick.

56. 26.6.72. W. Biggs, a former Alnwick schoolfriend.

57. 26.6.72. Lesbury; a village on the banks of the Aln, near Alnmouth.

58. 27.6.72. J. Hunter, an Alnwick friend.

59. 27.6.72. Howick, A coastal village in Northumberland, 5 miles NE of Alnwick.

60. 11.7.72. Samuel Reay; organist, b. Hexham 1822, d. Newark 1905; said to have been the first organist to arrange and play in church Mendelssohn's Wedding March from Shakespeare's *Midsummer Night's Dream*.

61. 20.7.72. The Chapel of the Nine Altars; the chapel of the East Transept in Durham Cathedral; completed in 1289 (Murray; Stranks). The windows were of clear glass before this date. It is interesting to find in the diary an eye-witness report of the putting in of the present bright-coloured Victorian stained glass in the Chapel of the Nine Altars. These windows present a striking feature of the far east-end of the long vista of the interior of the Cathedral.

62. 17.8.72. This was probably a temporary partition to screen off the work of scraping the white paint from the stone-work as noted on 4 Apr. 1872. The diary entry is hardly likely to refer to the erection of the new marble and alabaster choir-screen separating the choir from the nave, which Sir Gilbert Scott erected just about this time. T.H.C. would almost certainly have alluded to this as the choir-screen and not as a 'partition'.

63. 20.8.72. Sir John Goss; b. Hampshire 1800, d. London 1880; organist of St Paul's Cathedral, London and a composer of 'admirable church music' (Scholes). He published in 1833 *An Introduction to Harmony and Thorough-bass* (Grove). The section on the harmonisation of melodies is a useful one, and this is probably the work mentioned here. F.C.

64. 22.8.72. George M. Garrett (1834–97) organist and composer of church services (Scholes).

65. 24.8.72. Nicholson; a Cathedral chorister.

66. 26.8.72. Lampton (*recte*, Lambton); a parish on the River Wear six and a half miles north east of Durham city. Lambton Castle is the seat of the Earl of Durham, to whom the manor gives the title of viscount (Bartholomew).

67. 3.9.72. Broken Wall Walk; a favourite walk in Durham city. The ancient defence wall once completely surrounded the peninsula of the city. That part of the Wall running along the west side of the peninsula above the river became broken in older times through quarrying operations. A pathway known as Broken Wall Walk follows the line of the wall northwards from Prebends' Bridge, at a higher level, to Framwellgate Bridge (cf. Mee). It was a favourite walk in the city in the days of T.H.C.'s apprenticeship. Other parts of the wall are still visible, notably from the Water Gate at the south end of the peninsula to Kingsgate Bridge, and at one or two other places on the peninsula.

68. 4.9.72. Miss Greatorex was presumably either the daughter or the sister of the Precentor, Edward Greatorex. Thomas Greatorex, (who in this case would be her grandfather), was one-time organist of Westminster Abbey. It is reasonable to suppose that musical talent continued to manifest itself in this third generation of the Greatorex family.

69. 7.9.72. It was a well established tradition of the period that the church organist should be able to put right mechanical faults in the organ. I have often seen my father do this with the organ at St Mary's Cathedral, Edinburgh. F.C.

70. 8.9.72. Adolph Friedrich Hesse, b. Breslau 1809, d. there 1863; the son of an organ builder and a great organist; a particularly great player on the pedals of the organ. A complete collection of his organ works was edited by Charles Steggal, b. London 1826, d. there 1905; Professor, Royal Academy of Music (Grove).

71. 11.9.72. Mr Crament, his first teacher of musical theory at Alnwick. Cf. Introduction p. xviii.

72. 13.9.72. *Ouseley in E flat*; the setting in the key of E flat of the music for morning service composed by Sir F. A. G. Ouseley.

73. 13.9.72. Anthem, *Is it nothing to you all ye that pass by?* composed by Sir F. A. G. Ouseley.

74. 14.9.72. The organ at the church of St Mary-le-Bow, situated in the North Bailey; so called from the arch or 'bow' of its tower, which once spanned the street, leaving a roadway for carriages beneath (Murray).

75. 18.9.72. Henry Smart, b. London 1813, d. there 1879; composer of flowing effective organ music (Scholes).

76. 18.9.72. 'Stone's arrangements'; cannot be identified. From his early date it is unlikely that Robert Stone (1516–1613) can be intended.

77. 20.9.72. i.e. the Te Deum and Jubilate sung to anglican chants instead of to a composed setting.

78. 20.9.72. *The Lord will deliver*; an anthem composed by Maurice Greene, b. London *c.*1694, d. there 1755; organist of St. Paul's Cathedral and the Chapel Royal (Scholes).

79. 21.9.72. 'Nicholson blew'; i.e. he pumped the bellows of the organ with the long bellows hand-lever. Water engines or electric organ-blowers had not yet come into common use.

80. 22.9.72. Carl Czerny; b. Vienna 1791, d. there 1857; was a pupil of Beethoven and teacher of Lizst. Scholes describes him as 'the world's champion writer of piano studies'. It was probably one of Czerny's piano pieces that T.H.C. played as an out-voluntary.

81. 23.9.72. This is of course the well-known opening recitative from Handel's *Messiah.* It seems rather remarkable that T.H.C. with his already considerable knowledge of choral music should not have encountered the piece before. The time was to come when in later later life he was to conduct the *Messiah* every New Year's Day for thirty consecutive years, as conductor of the Edinburgh Royal Choral Union.

82. 24.9.72. Wortley; not identified, possibly one of the Cathedral choristers.

83. 25.9.72. Rogers in D; this almost certainly refers to Benjamin Rogers, b. Windsor 1614, d. Oxford 1698. He composed a good deal of church music, some of it still in regular use (Scholes).

84. 25.9.72. *O Pray for the Peace of Jerusalem*, anthem by Henry Purcell (b. London *c.*1658, d. there 1695). He is too well-known to require further annotation.

85. 25.9.72. 'The large Boyce score'; a collection of church music published by William Boyce (b. London 1710, d. there 1779) in 'open score', with G.C. and F clefs, under the title of *Cathedral Music.* It proves a testing exercise in score reading for the musician. Scholes says of Boyce that 'his work upon this [*Cathedral Music*] has been recognised as the erection of a national monument, and the execution of a public service'.

86. 27.9.72. *Call to Remembrance*; anthem by Richard Farrant, cf. 29 May 1873.

87. 30.9.72. T.H.C.'s father, as said in the Introduction, was headmaster of the Duke's School Alnwick. The Duchess here mentioned is the Duchess of Northumberland. T.H.C.'s father, Thomas Collinson, was a close and trusted confidant of the Duke and Duchess.

88. 3.10.72. J. L. Dussek, b. Bohemia 1760, d. 1812; was a well-known composer of piano music including sonatas (Scholes).

89. 8.10.72. The month was then October, by which time brambles (blackberries) lose their flavour. It was a popular saying that 'in October the Devil enters into the brambles'!

90. 8.10.72. Mr Rowton's Cradle Songs—cannot be identified.
91. 9.10.72. Probably one of Mendelssohn's Six Preludes and Fugues for pianoforte, Op. 35.
92. 11.10.72. Cherubini, Maria Luigi Carlo Z.S.; b. Florence 1760, d. Paris, 1842 (Scholes). The diary entry refers to his 'Course of Counterpoint and Fugue' which was the standard work of the period on the subject.
93. 14.10.72. Beethoven's pianoforte sonata Op. 10, No. 3.
94. 18.10.72. Chillingham, a village and estate in Northumberland. Chillingham Park is famous for its herd of indigenous white cattle.
95. 19.10.72. The Prince and Princess of Wales; later to become King Edward VII and Queen Alexandra.
96. 24.10.72. Ushaw College; dedicated to St Cuthbert; four miles west of Durham; founded in 1804 to replace the dispossessed seminary for Roman Catholic priests at Douai in Flanders. It is said that the greater part of the north of England was supplied with Roman Catholic clergy from the college (Murray).
97. 24.10.72. A 'double' in organ parlance means a set of pipes or 'stop' of double the length of the other pipes which are of eight feet scale, i.e. the 'double' is of sixteen feet scale, giving the pitch of an octave below the others.
98. 25.10.72. George M. Garrett; b. Winchester, 1834, d. Cambridge 1897; organist of St John's College Cambridge.
99. 26.10.72. The Durham Choral Union.
100. 28.10.72. William Rae, b. London 1827, d. Newcastle upon Tyne 1903; organist to the Corporation of Newcastle upon Tyne. He ran a series of choral and orchestral concerts at Newcastle.
101. 31.10.72. Durham Castle; erected by William the Conqueror in 1072 to guard the neck of the peninsula formed by the curve of the River Wear. The Castle was given over to the installation and use of Durham University by Bishop Van Mildert in 1833 (Muirhead).
102. 31.10.72. The students of Durham University College, situated in the Castle.
103. 6.11.72. Carl Heinrich Graun, b. Saxony 1703 or 1704, d. Berlin 1759. He was Musical Director at Potsdam to King Frederick the Great (Scholes).
104. 6.11.72. Hetton, a village in north County Durham.
105. 13.11.72. Fourth order of two-part counterpoint; Counterpoint is the art of writing one or more melodies against another, (the latter often a given melody or subject) so that the whole makes a satisfactory musical progression. Such a given melody or subject is often known as a *canto fermo.* For purposes of progressive study, counterpoint is divided into five orders, each of increasing complexity. These five orders may be worked in two or more musical parts. The student is usually required to write in up to four or perhaps five musical parts; but in actual compositional practice the number of contrapuntal parts is only limited by the ingenuity of the composer.
106. 25.12.72. Giovanni Battista Pergolesi; b. Jesi, Italy, 1710, d. Naples 1736; composer of operas and much sacred music (Scholes).
107. 26.12.72. Alnwick friends.

1873

1. 1.1.73. Since 1693 Durham Cathedral has possessed a peal of eight bells. Cf. also 8 October 1873 and 11 July 1873. The number was increased to ten bells in 1980.
2. 15.1.73. Modulation; the art of moving or 'modulating' from one key to another in music.
3. 31.1.73. Wesley in F. Music for morning service; this could be the composition of either Samuel Wesley, b. Bristol 1766, d. 1837; or of Samuel Sebastian Wesley, his natural son, b. London 1810, d. Gloucester 1876.

4. 3.2.73. Gray & Davidson; a well-known firm of organ builders in London.
5. 4.2.73. J. Marshall, photographer, Alnwick.
6. 6.2.73. Thomas Tallis, *c.*1505–85. (Scholes); Gentleman of the Chapel Royal under Henry VIII and Queen Elizabeth.
7. 11.2.73. This is of interest as being apparently the Inaugural Meeting of the Durham Musical Society. This receives confirmation in the *Durham Advertiser* of 4 February 1876 (i.e. three years later), which refers to the *3rd Annual General Meeting* of the Society, held 1 February 1876. Though it anticipates the chronicle of events, it may be appropriate to add here from the account of the meeting of 1876 that 'Mr George Salkeld read the following report—. . . your committee desire to express their thanks to the following gentlemen—to Mr Collinson for his most able services as accompanyist (*sic*) both at the Society's rehearsals and at the concerts'. . . .
8. 12.2.73. Anthem by Thomas Attwood Walmisley, b. London 1814, d. Hastings 1856.
9. 16.2.73. Mozart's Twelfth Mass; probably K262 in C, composed in 1776 (Grove).
10. 16.2.73. Fred; the elder of T.H.C.'s two half-brothers. At that time he was training to be a chemist. He later became a surgeon and a distinguished member of the FRCS Edinburgh.
11. 16.2.73. Sam; his other half-brother.
12. 21.2.73. G. B. Arnold, b. Petworth, Sussex, 1832, d. 1902; organist of Winchester Cathedral 1865; composer of church music (West).
13. 22.2.73. The Revd Thomas Rogers, Precentor of Durham.
14. 25.2.73. Charles Moore, his first organ teacher at Alnwick. Cf. Introduction.
15. 25.2.73. The Sanctuary Knocker, late twelfth-century Norman; a fugitive from justice could claim sanctuary within the Cathedral. Upon knocking upon the Great North Door by means of the Sanctuary Knocker, the fugitive was immediately admitted to the safety of the church by two monks whose duty it was to be constantly on the watch in the chamber above for such an appeal. The fantasy of the pancakes was without doubt of later provenance!
16. 2.3.73. One of Rinck's fugues; cf. 29 Jan. 1872.
17. 10.3.73. Friedrich Heinrich Himmel, b. Brandenburg 1765, d. Berlin 1814. *Incline Thine ear* was the best known of his anthems (Scholes).
18. 11.3.73. Anthem by James Kent, b. Winchester 1700, d. there 1776 (Grove).
19. 12.3.73. Anthem by Robert Creyghton or Creighton, b. 1636 (or '37), d. Wells 1734 (Grove).
20. 13.3.73 Edward John Hopkins; b. London 1818, d. there 1901; Organist of the Temple Church, London; a composer of anthems and services that are much valued in English cathedrals and churches (Scholes).
21. 13.3.73. *Try me O God*; anthem by James Nares; b. Middlesex 1715, d. London 1783; organist of York Minster and of the Chapel Royal (Scholes).
22. 15.3.73. John Marsh, b. Dorking 1752, d. Chichester 1828.; cultured musical amateur; his compositions include some church music (Grove).
23. 17.3.73. Halle's band; this is of course the Hallé Orchestra.
24. 20.3.73. William Croft, b. Warwickshire 1678, d. Bath 1727 (Scholes).
25. 23.3.73. *Zampa*; the opera by Louis J. F. Herold. Almost certainly it is the overture that is meant here.
26. 29.3.73. Schubert's *March Heroic*; probably one of the *Trois Marches Héroiques* for pianoforte for four hands.
27. 29.3.73. Grand Rondo; one of the same composer's *Rondos for four hands.*
28. 1.4.73. Charles Stroud, b. *c.*1705, d. 1726. He is remembered for his one anthem, *Hear my Prayer* (Oscar Thomson).
29. 2.4.73. The Revd Dr. J. B. Dykes, b. Hull 1823, d. St Leonards 1876. Vicar and organist of St Oswald's Church, Durham; a minor canon of Durham Cathedral.
30. 3.4.73. The *Durham Advertiser* regularly printed the programmes of the Durham Musical Society, immediately below the Cathedral list of music. The programme of this concert appears as follows.

DURHAM MUSICAL SOCIETY

Concert, Thursday May 1—Programme

Chorus—In these delightful [groves to dwell]—Purcell
Part-Song—Oh, fly with me—Mendelssohn
Glee—From Oberon—Stevens
Chorus—May no rash intruder—Handel
Song—The moonlight glisten (*sic*).—Smart
Part-Song—On a Lake—Mendelssohn
Pianoforte Duet—Schubert
Part-Song—May-Day—Muller

March—Men of Harlech!
Duetto—*Soffrina nil pianto*—Donizetti
Chorus—Galatea, dry thy tears—Handel
Song—Oh, beauteous daughter—Beethoven
Part-Song—The Lark—Mendelssohn
Part-Song—The Hunter's farewell—Mendelssohn
Market Chorus—(Masaniello)—Auber

God Save the Queen

Philip Armes, Mus.Doc., Conductor

31. 5.4.73. The new organ; in 1873 Henry Willis commenced to erect a new organ to replace the old 'Father Smith' organ which had served the Cathedral—with various improvements and additions by other organ-builders—since 1686 or thereabouts; according to T.H.C. the work of erecting the new organ in the Cathedral commenced on 5 April 1873. By 19 April, only fourteen days later, he records that the new organ was in use.
32. 7.4.73. His brother Fred's qualifying examination as a chemist, prior to his entering the study of Medicine, in which he was to have a distinguished career.
33. 10.4.73. The selection from Bach's Passion Music (which version of the Passion is not stated, but probably the St Matthew Passion) was performed by the Durham Musical Society.
34. 22.4.73. The *Durham Advertiser* names the unfortunate man as Mr Charles Winter Brown of 4 Cross Street, i.e. next door to T.H.C.'s lodgings with the Lawsons at No. 3. He was stated to be a solicitor's clerk, aged thirty-one years.
35. 25.4.73. William Thomas Best; cf. 9 Apr. 1872. In addition to arranging Handel's choruses for organ, Best published a fine edition of the organ works of Bach.
36. 26.4.73. Tuning the reeds; the pitch of the reed pipes of the organ is constantly affected by changes of temperature as well as by the actual use of the pipes in playing, and they require frequent adjustment to keep them in tune. Many organists, particularly of the older school are able to do this themselves. A tuning rod of metal is used to tap gently the head of the tuning wire to lengthen or shorten the length of the vibrating part of the tongue of the reed. F.C.
37. 30.4.73. 'The old organ', built *c.*1683 by Bernard Schmidt ('Father Smith') b. Germany 1630, d. London 1708. The incident here related in the diary should be of considerable interest in organ history.
38. 1.5.73. The *Durham Advertiser* of 2 May 1873 gives the following: 'The first private rehearsal of the members of this Society (The Durham Musical Society) took place in the New Town Hall last evening (Thursday). The room was crowded to excess by the *élite* (*sic* in italics) of the city, who had received an invitation to be present at this inaugurative essay of the Society. The baton was wielded by Dr Armes.
39. 7.5.73. 'We cleared the swell', i.e. the pipes of the swell organ.

40. 10.5.73. The title of the anthem sung at the afternoon service at the Cathedral.

41. 16.5.73. Birtley; a village 5½ miles SE of Gateshead; or it could have been the village with the same name in South Northumberland, on the River Tyne.

42. 21.5.73. The choruses in Judas Maccabaeus.

43. 23.5.73. 'The riflemen', i.e. of the Durham Militia.

44. 27.5.73. *O sing unto the Lord a new song!*, anthem composed by Maurice Greene; cf. 20 Nov. 1872.

45. 29.5.73. Singing from the Tower; the following is taken with acknowledgement from *Durham Cathedral* by James Wall, BA, former Precentor of the Cathedral, published Durham 1930, republished by Raphael Tuck & Sons, Ltd. 1955. 'After evensong [on Royal Oak Day] the choir climbs to the top of the central tower [of the Cathedral] and sings three anthems from three different sides;—*Lord, for thy tender mercy's sake, lay not our sins to our charge* (Richard Farrant) towards the south; *Therefore with angels and archangels* (Vincent Novello) towards the east; and *Give peace in our time, O Lord* (W. H. Calcott) towards the north. The field of battle [i.e. the Battle of Red Hills, 1346] lay on the west. No anthem is sung facing this way, on the theory either that the monks for sentimental or for more practical reasons could not bring themselves to face the scene of the fighting, or that as they were originally praying for help, they could not expect any reinforcements from that side, and so confined their devotions to potentially more profitable directions.' cf. 29.5.72.

46. 29.5.73. Richard Farrant b. *c.*1525-30, d. London 1580; was organist of St George's Chapel Windsor. The anthem above specified however is now thought to have been composed by John Hilton, or perhaps Christopher Tye (Scholes); (West) T.H.C. evidently also doubts its ascription to Farrant.

47. 29.5.73. Vincent Novello, 1781–1861; composed much church music and revived much more (Scholes).

48. 29.5.73. William H. Calcott, b. London 1807, d. there 1882 (Scholes). In a lighter vein, it may be added here that the abbreviating of the titles of anthems as in T.H.C's entry *Lord for thy tender*—Farrant, was an amusing quirk or 'custom of the profession' of the compiler of church music lists. It often led (possibly deliberately) to comic absurdities, as with the anthem by E. J. Hopkins, *I will wash away all tears* (or some such title) which would appear in the music list as *I will wash, Hopkins*, the comma inserted or omitted according to the sense of humour of the compiler. Perhaps the height of such playfulness was reached in *My God, Blow*(!) sounding like an agonised exhortation to the organ-blower to provide more wind, rather than the title of an anthem, by the composer John Blow.

49. 13.6.73. Henry Aldrich, b. London 1648, d. Oxford 1710; Dean of Christ Church, Oxford; composer of church and secular music (Grove).

50. 9.7.73. The seat of Palace of the Bishops of Durham since the twelfth century has been at Bishop Auckland, County Durham, twelve miles to the south west of Durham City.

51. 11.7.73. The great west window of the Cathedral. It is known as the Jesse Window from the design depicting the 'rute of Jessei' (root of Jesse) (cf. 'Rites of Durham' *c.*1593) a favourite theme of the Middle Ages picturing the ancestors and foretellers of Christ. The Jesse Window, in decorated style consisting of seven lights with foliated tracery in the head, was built by Prior Forcer or Fosser, about the fourteenth century, to replace the original Norman windows at the west end of the Cathedral. The window was originally of painted glass which later became destroyed. The present glass was the gift of the then Dean of Durham; it was put in in 1867. In the diary account, T.H.C. and his brother Sam and friends had gone along the triforium to the extreme west end of the Cathedral, close to the Jesse Window.

52. 11.7.73. The great Galilee Bell which was originally hung in the northwest Galilee Tower, was tolled in the monastic days when sanctuary was claimed by offenders. There were four bells in the northwest tower, but these had gone out of use at the Dissolution, and in 1563 were moved to the central tower. The Galilee Bell, now known as the Bell of St Cuthbert, was recast in 1693 along with the other six bells in the central belfry above the lantern, to make the former peal of eight bells. Cf. 'Bells past and present in Durham Cathedral' (leaflet published by Durham Cathedral).

53. 11.7.73. i.e. to the top of the central tower.
54. 12.7.73. Fencehouses; a hamlet 5½ miles NE of Durham.
55. 20.7.73. Mrs Rushforth was the mother of Thomas Collinson's first wife, Mary Anne Rushforth.
56. 20.7.73. St Margaret's Church, between Crossgate and South Street; almost entirely Norman (Muirhead); one of the historic churches of Durham (Mee).
57. 20.7.73. 'Great open', i.e. the open diapason in the 'great' organ.
58. 20.7.73. 'Swell reeds', i.e. the reed pipes in the 'swell' organ.
59. 6.8.73. Castle Eden, northeast County Durham; beauty spot on the sea-coast.
60. 8.8.73. Macfarren, Sir George; b. London 1813, d. there 1887 (Grove). The work referred to was almost certainly Macfarren's *Rudiments of Harmony* (1860).
61. 11.8.73. A grammatical slip which occurs more than once in the diary!
62. 11.8.73. Muzio Clementi; b. Rome 1752, d. Evesham, Worcs. 1832. His *Gradus ad Parnassum*, a book of studies for the pianoforte, was a popular and much used work in its day, and is still by no means forgotten (Scholes).
63. 19.8.73. 'L.M.'; i.e. Long Metre, a metre consisting of four lines of eight syllables—a common hymn-tune metre.
64. 25.8.73. The Round Window; above the Chapel of the Nine Altars, at the far east end of the Cathedral.
65. 29.9.73. Mr Edwin; cannot be identified; probably a friend of the family as the *locale* here is Alnwick. The vehicle used for the drive would of course be horse-drawn at that period.
66. 1.10.73. Hulne Abbey; cf. 21 June 1872.
67. 1.10.73. Charles François Gounod, b. Paris 1818, d. near there, 1893.
68. 2.10.73. Beethoven, Sonata in C; probably the *Waldstein Sonata*, Op. 53.
69. 16.10.73. Joseph Haydn's oratorio, *The Creation*.
70. 20.10.73. Chester-le-Street; town, 6 miles N of Durham; ancient Roman fortress on the Roman road from Binchester to Newcastle. The coffin and remains of St Cuthbert were laid here in 875 and remained there for 113 years before being carried first to Ripon and then to Durham. The present church in Chester-le-Street was built by Bishop Egelric 2 years before the Norman Conquest, i.e. in 1064.

1874

1. 18.3.74. Hans von Bülow, b. Dresden 1830, d. Cairo 1894 (Scholes); the famous pianist and conductor; married Liszt's daughter Cosima, who left him for Richard Wagner.
2. 18.3.74. All these places are in the western environs of Durham city.
3. 21.3.74. The *Musical Standard*; the musical periodical of that name.
4. 27.3.74. Ouseley's *Harmony*; cf. 15 October 1872.
5. 4.4.74. Counterpoint in two parts which may be satisfactorily 'inverted' at the interval of a tenth.
6. 11.4.74. The factory of the well-known Durham firm of organ-builders, Harrison & Harrison. The Mr Harrison mentioned was Thomas Hugh Harrison, who had moved his business from Rochdale in Lancashire to Durham two years before, at the encouragement of Dr J. M. Dykes (cf. brochure by Harrison & Harrison, 1981).
7. 11.4.74. Sherbourne. This is a mis-spelling of Sherburn (Durham). The organ was intended for the church there. (Information from Mr. Cuthbert Harrison of Messrs Harrison & Harrison).

8. 13.4.74. There are no compositions with the title of 'nocturne' to be found in the list of Schubert's works unless one allows his arrangement of W. Matiegka's 'Notturna' for four instruments. cf. The New Grove Vol. 16, p 807. It could have been a Chopin nocturne. If so, it is, rather remarkably, the only example of Chopin's music mentioned in the diary.
9. 23.4.74. The Banks, i.e. river banks; a favourite laid-out walk and beauty spot in Durham.
10. 29.4.74. Charles Vincent, a former choirboy at Durham Cathedral. He was born at Houghton-le-Spring, Co Durham in 1852 and died at Monte Carlo in 1954. In 1876/78, two years later than his meetings with T.H.C. chronicled in the diary, he studied music at Leipzig Conservatoire. His younger brother, George Frederick Vincent, b. 1855, was already at Leipzig at the time mentioned in the diary, where he studied at the Conservatoire from 1874–6. Charles Vincent wrote *Scoring for an Orchestra* (1897, privately printed).
11. 1.5.74. Castle Howard; North Riding, Yorks; then the seat of the Earl of Carlisle (Bartholomew, 1904).
12. 2.6.74. Dick's microscope; Dick is probably T.H.C.'s cousin Richard, mentioned on 8 October 1871.
13. 4.6.74. Hector Berlioz, b. near Grenoble 1803, d. Paris 1869; *A Treatise on Modern Instrumentation and Orchestration* (1843).
14. 5.6.74. Mr Greenwell; one of the party agents in the parliamentary election.
15. 6.6.74. 'Touched up the flute and reeds', i.e. put them in tune.
16. 12.6.74. Henry Willis; famous organ-builder, known as 'Father Willis'. Following negotiations with the Dean and Chapter of Durham Cathedral, Willis erected a still newer organ than the one already referred to in the diary on 5 Apr. 1873.
17. 28.6.74. J. S. Bach's *St Anne's Fugue* so called from the similarity of the fugue subject to the first line of William Croft's hymn tune, *St Anne.* William Croft was born in Warwickshire in 1678 and died at Bath in 1727 (Grove). He was thus very roughly contemporary with J. S. Bach (1685–1750).
18. 29.6.74. Sir George Macfarren; his *Six Lectures on Harmony* (1867) was a companion work to his *Rudiments of Harmony* (1860).
19. 14.7.74. I am indebted to the Astronomer Royal for Scotland, Professor M. S. Longair and to Mr Russell D. Eberst of the UK Schmidt Telescope Unit, Royal Observatory, Blackford Hill, Edinburgh, for the following note:

    'The comet seen by your father was undoubtedly 1874 III (3) Comet Coggia. It was the first of two comets discovered by Coggia in that year. At the time of observation, the comet was about 35 million miles from the Earth, and about 70 million miles from the Sun. Observing on the same date, the French astronomer D'Arrest noted the brightness as being magnitude + 1.2, which means that it was as bright as Pollux (in Gemini) which is the 17th brightest star in the sky. It was last observed on 19 October 1874, and will not be seen again for many years since its orbital period is many thousands of years.'
20. 15.7.74. The Church of St Nicholas, being situated in the Market Place in Durham City, is often known as 'The Market Church'. cf. 7.10.71.
21. 15.7.74. Mr Stimpson; probably the regular organist of the church.
22. 26.7.74. Adolph Bernhard Marx, b. Halle 1795, d. Berlin 1866; published a long series of learned writings, chiefly on musical aesthetics. He helped to elucidate Beethoven to the public, and he encouraged the young Mendelssohn (Scholes).
23. 28.7.74. Ripon Cathedral was closed in June 1862 for alterations and restorations over a considerable period. As restoration proceeded, special celebratory services were held to mark the reopening of successive parts of the building. Thus in 1869, the Choir was reopened for worship. In October 1872 (not however mentioned in the diary) the reopening of the nave was celebrated by another special service. The diary entry of 28 July 1874 chronicles a further service to mark the completion of further alterations. (Information from Mr G. E. Thorpe, Canons' Verger and Parish Clerk of Ripon Minster).
24. 11.8.74. Roker; watering place with promenade and Pier, NE County Durham, near Sunderland.

25. 18.8.74. This refers to a prospective appointment as organist to one of the churches in Cornhill, London, probably either St Michael's, Cornhill, or the Church of St Peter-upon-Cornhill. John Whitehead did not get or take this appointment.
26. 20.8.74. Litolff's edition; these are now in my possession. F.C.
27. 21.8.74. The little boy was Arthur Harrison, born in 1868; the son of Thomas Hugh Harrison, organ builder, Durham. Arthur Harrison received music lessons first from T.H.C. and later from Dr Armes. He was appointed organist of St Giles' Church, Durham in 1881 at the age of thirteen. He and his brother Harry succeeded to the control of the business of Harrison & Harrison in the 1890s. He is commemorated by a stained-glass window in the Cathedral.
28. 31.8.74. An engine driven by water for operating the bellows of an organ. The engine was for use at the factory of Harrison & Harrison.
29. 3.9.74. Vox Celestis and Echo Salicional; the names of two organ stops of the swell or solo organ. Salicional derives from *salix*, willow, and the organ stop of that name possesses a soft reedy tone intended to resemble that of a pipe of willow (O.E.D.).
30. 6.9.74. Miss Langley, Miss Lincoln and Miss Chambers; friends of T.H.C's brother Sam. Sam, the future parson, was obviously the one of the three brothers, most interested in the opposite sex! Cf. also p 80, 18.2.75.
31. 13.9.74. The rector of Bury; probably of the church of St Mary, Bury, an early foundation (Encyclo. Brit.).
32. 26.9.74. Gray & Davison, organ builders, London.
33. 5.10.74. *Semiramide*; an operatic story set by a number of different composers. The diary reference is almost certainly to the opera of that name by Rossini.
34. 5.10.74. A mistake! Beethoven's first symphony is in C.
35. 13.10.74. John Pyke Hullah, b. Worcester 1812, d. London 1884. He instituted a system of sight-singing which became very popular in the mid-nineteenth century (Scholes).
36. 19.10.74. *La Gazza Ladra*, by Rossini; produced at Milan, 31 May 1817, and London 1821 (Grove).
37. 29.10.74. Edward John Hopkins, b. London 1818, d. there 1901; organist of the Temple Church London; composer of church music much valued in English cathedrals (Scholes). cf. 13.3.73.
38. 6.11.74. There were four members of the Gibbons family, all noted as composers of church music, extending from 1570 to 1676. The best known is Orlando Gibbons, organist of the Chapel Royal and of Westminster Abbey (Scholes).
39. 6.11.74. Charles Vincent, cf. 29 Apr. 1874.
40. 13.11.74. Mendelssohn's oratorio *Elijah*, composed in 1846; first performed at the Birmingham Festival in 1847, the year of Mendelssohn's death (Scholes; Grove).
41. 23.11.74. W. Biggs; his Alnwick friend before-mentioned.

1875

1. 4.1.75. This refers to the bells at one of the churches at Alnwick.
2. 5.1.75. James Alexander Hamilton, b. London 1785, d. there 1845; wrote a long series of catechisms on musical instruments, many of which have passed through numerous editions (Grove).
3. 6.1.75. *Arise, shine, for thy light has come!*; anthem by Maurice Greene; cf. 20 Sept. 1872.
4. 8.1.75. The Revd Thomas Rogers, Precentor of Durham.
5. 12.1.75. Charles Moore, T.H.C's first organ teacher.
6. 13.1.75. Sir Frederick Ouseley; cf. 15 Oct. 1872.
7. 15.1.75. Probably John Frederick Bridge, b. Oldsbury 1844, d. Westminster, 1924; appointed deputy organist of Westminster Abbey in 1875, succeeding to the organistship in 1882. Popularly known among his fellow organists as 'Westminster Bridge'.

Alternatively the diary might refer to the younger brother of the above, Joseph Cox Bridge, b. Rochester 1853, d. St Albans 1929; became organist of Chester Cathedral 1877. Appointed Professor of Music at Durham, 1908.

8. 17.1.75. Berthold Tours; b. Rotterdam 1838, d. London 1807; published neat and effective music for the English Church (Scholes).
9. 18.1.75. i.e. pedals as for the organ. These were in frequent use for practising organ music with pedal part, on the piano at home. Mr Richardson was the organist of St Margaret's Church, Durham.
10. 19.1.75. Joseph Haydn's oratorio, *The Seasons* to be performed by the Durham Choral Society later in the year.
11. 21.1.75. 'It will not be sung, most likely'—early disillusionment!
12. 21.1.75. The Duke's School, Alnwick.
13. 21.1.75. The full title of the song is, *If doughty deeds my lady please,* music by Arthur Sullivan; one of several settings by different composers of the song-lyric by Graham of Gartmore.
14. 23.1.75. J. M. Crament; T.H.C.'s early teacher, at Alnwick, of musical theory.
15. 26.1.75. The Bailey; an ancient street running along the east side of the Durham peninsula above the river. Bow Church is in The Bailey.
16. 27.1.75. The two little Miss Holdens; cannot be identified.
17. 30.1.75. Presumably rehearsals of *The Seasons* by the Durham Musical Society is meant.
18. 31.1.75. 'The St Cuthbert's organ affair'. This is the first mention of a strange and unexplained incident which was to lead to T.H.C. leaving St Cuthbert's and ceasing to work there. It should be read in conjunction with the entries for 14 Feb. 1875 and 7 Mar. 1875, at which date T.H.C. ceased his work at St Cuthbert's.
19. 8.2.75. Mr Downs; not identifiable; probably an executive member of the Durham Musical Society.
20. 8.2.75. *Faust*; the opera by Charles Francois Gounod, b. Paris 1818, d. near there, 1893. The opera was first produced in 1859.
21. 14.2.75. This note should be read in conjunction with the 'St. Cuthbert's organ affair' (31 Jan. 1875). T.H.C. was given notice that he was to finish at St Cuthbert's on the first Sunday in March (7 Mar. 1875, which see).
22. 24.2.75. Mr J. Baillie Hamilton; not mentioned as a writer on musical subjects in the standard reference books. Baillie-Hamilton is the family name of the Earl of Haddington.
23. 7.3.75. T.H.C. finishes at St Cuthbert's. He gives no reason in the diary for his having, as he says, 'suddenly' ceased to assist at the organ and choir practices at St Cuthbert's, beyond Donkin's statement on 14 Feb. 1875 that 'he could not get matters arranged with the Doctor', and his own diary entry of 31 Jan. 1875 that the St Cuthbert's organ affair 'just happened from a mistake or misunderstanding of Mr Ridley's'. Whatever the explanation of the affair, T.H.C. happily seems to have been quite unperturbed by this turn of events. Two months later, on 10 Apr. 1875, T.H.C. records that 'Mr Donkin wants me to teach his son on the organ'.
24. 10.3.75. Beethoven's *Moonlight Sonata,* op. 27. no. 2.
25. 20.3.75. This is the only reference to the music of Brahms in the diary.
26. 27.3.75. Coxhoe; a country seat 5½ miles south of Durham.
27. 4.5.75. Pierson's *Roman Dirge*; Henry Hugo Pierson (originally 'Pearson'); b. Oxford 1815, d. Leipzig 1873. He went to Germany in his early twenties where he became known to Mendelssohn, Schumann, and other leading composers. He was for a time Professor of Music at Edinburgh University, but soon returned to Germany. His oratorios, operas, songs and instrumental pieces (some published under the name of 'Edgar Mansfeldt') had success in his day (Scholes). The concert, fully reported in the *Durham Advertiser* of 7 May 1875, is described as the sixth private concert of the Durham Musical Society, of which there appears to have been two such in each yearly session of the Society. The hall is described as being, 'filled by the fashionable and *élite* of the city in full dress'—a word already used in a previous notice of the Society's private concerts. The notice recounts

that 'Mr Collinson, pupil of Dr Armes, accompanied on the piano, and displayed a wonderful mastery over that instrument, more especially in the selection from the *Midsummer Night's Dream* and in the *Hungarian Dances* where in conjunction with Dr Armes a most pleasing piece of musical talent was displayed, which was heartily applauded'.

28. 15.5.75. Towlaw, a small town 8 miles NW of Bishop Auckland, Co Durham.

29. 15.5.75. Mr Richardson, who conducted the Wooley brass band, was the organist of St Margaret's Church, Durham.

30. 19.6.75. The brother was Reginald Harrison, T. H. Harrison's fourth son (information from Cuthbert Harrison, Chairman of Directors, Messrs Harrison & Harrison).

31. 29.6.75. J. Gomperts Montefiore, author of a *History of England in Verse* (1876); not mentioned in musical reference books.

INDEX